RESCUE

Helen Chapman

NASEN House, 4/5 Amber Business Village, Amber Close, Amington, Tamworth, Staffordshire, B77 4RP

Rising Stars UK Ltd.
7 Hatchers Mews, Bermondsey Street, London SE1 3GS
www.risingstars-uk.com

Published 2011
Reprinted 2013 (twice), 2014

Cover design: Burville-Riley Partnership
Illustrations: Bill Greenhead for Illustration Ltd. / iStock
Text design and typesetting: Geoff Rayner
Publisher: Gill Budgell
Publishing manager: Sasha Morton
Editorial consultants: Lorraine Petersen and Dee Reid
Editorial: Jane Wood

British Library Cataloguing in Publication Data.
A CIP record for this book is available from the British Library.

ISBN: 978-1-84680-981-1

Printed in the UK by Ashford Colour Press Ltd, Gosport, Hampshire

CONTENTS

MEET THE GANG-STARS!

Jacky

Tom

Natalie

4

Zeke

Aaron

?

Callum

Becca

Claire

Name:
Claire

Special skill:
Classical ballet

Good at:
Being graceful; working hard; spreading sunshine and happiness

Not so good at:
Understanding modern dance

Other info:
A real girlie girl who wears a lot of pink and loves the elegance of classical ballet.

PROFILES

Name:
Callum

Special skill:
Pop singing

Good at:
Showing off

Not so good at:
Thinking about anyone but himself

Other info:
He's got the looks, the voice and the talent, and a massive ego. He's his own biggest fan, and he counts on his cousin Aaron to be his next biggest fan.

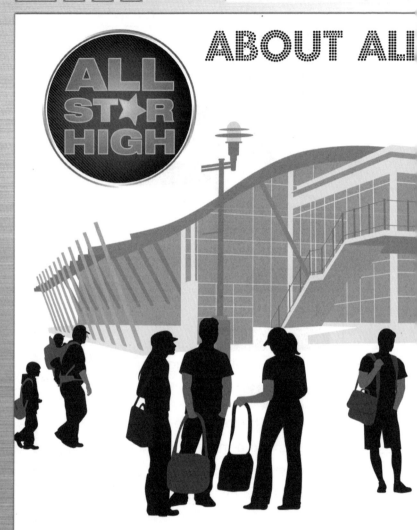

Do you want to be a star?
Then ALL STAR HIGH SCHOOL
is the place for YOU.
We will make you
a star.

Musicians,

dancers,

actors:

come see us now!

Don't miss out!

CHAPTER

Callum Murphy hated coming to school on a Saturday morning.

'I should be in bed,' he grumbled. But as the lead actor in the school's next show he had to be at **rehearsal**.

He was half asleep on the bus. But as soon as he got off the bus outside All Star High he was wide awake. Something was wrong. A small group of people were standing by the gates. They looked like they were waiting for something. Then he saw Claire Stevens. She looked really worried.

Callum and Claire were both in the Gang-Stars. The Gang-Stars always helped each other. They had first met at an under-12s music club. It was so great to meet up again at high school that they started a gang.

'What's going on?' Callum wondered. He walked across the road and went up to Claire. 'What's wrong?' he asked. 'We're only here to rehearse. You look as if there's a disaster.'

'I chose All Star High because it's the best **performing arts** school for dancers,' said Claire.

'And I chose it because it's the best school for actors and singers,' said Callum. He was puzzled. 'So what's the problem?'

'The Talent Academy is the problem,' said Claire.

The Talent Academy was a new performing arts school. It had just opened in the same town. The Academy was going to be great.

Everybody said so. It had brand-new everything including its own film studio and a full size theatre with a revolving stage!

'What if the Talent Academy becomes better than All Star High?' said Claire. 'Then their students will get all the best jobs and become famous.'

When people in the **entertainment** industry wanted a new young singer, dancer, musician or actor they always came to All Star High first. Callum and Claire didn't want that to change.

'Then all the best students would leave All Star High and go to the Talent Academy instead,' Claire went on. 'And if All Star High lost too many students, it would have to close down.'

'But why are you thinking about the Talent Academy now?' asked Callum. 'It has only just opened. It's too soon to know if it's going to be a problem.'

Claire nodded towards the group of people. 'The Talent Academy has an **open day** today. All these people have turned up here by mistake.'

'So send them away,' said Callum.

'No, I have an idea,' said Claire. 'I'm going to rescue our school. I'm going to give everyone a tour of All Star High. Then these visitors may decide to send their kids here.'

'It won't work,' said Callum. 'It's Saturday, everything is locked.'

'Not everything. The Main Hall is open, and the music rooms and dance studios,' said Claire. 'Come on, Callum. Are you going to help me or not?'

'No, I'm not,' said Callum. He walked over to the group of people standing by the gate. 'There's no open day here. You're at the wrong school,' he said, and he pointed to the big All Star High sign.

Some people started to leave but other people stayed. They had come a long way to see the Academy.

'No, this is the right place,' said a

woman and she handed Callum a flier. 'This is 651 Main Street, which is the address on the flier.'

Claire nudged Callum. 'There must have been a printing error,' she whispered. 'Come on, Callum. You're the best actor in the school. Act like a tour guide.'

A **stretch limousine** pulled up at the gate. The driver got out, opened the side doors and stood back. A skinny woman wearing dark glasses, and two teenagers got out.

Claire nudged Callum again. 'That's Zane and Zara Benson,' she said. 'They won that **reality show**, *Who's Going* *to be a Star?'*

Claire and Callum stood and watched as people got the twins' **autographs**.

Mrs Benson walked up to Claire and Callum.

'Ginger and I are here for the open day,' she said.

Claire and Callum looked at each other. Who or what was Ginger? Was someone else going to get out of the limousine?

'Good morning Mrs Benson,' they said politely.

Mrs Benson frowned. 'Aren't you forgetting someone?' she said.

'Er ...' Claire and Callum looked

around. Then they heard a whimper and looked down. There in Mrs Benson's handbag was a small fluffy dog.

Callum turned and glared at Claire. 'I'm not saying "good morning" to a dog!' he whispered.

'Good morning, Ginger,' said Claire sweetly. She nudged Callum. Callum gave in.

'Good morning, Ginger,' he mumbled.

Mrs Benson explained. 'I want Zane and Zara to go to the best performing arts school in the country.'

Claire saw her chance. 'Come with

us,' she said, as she grabbed Callum's arm and pulled him closer. 'We'll show you around.'

'What are you doing?' hissed Callum.

'We're not doing anything wrong and we haven't lied,' said Claire.

Mrs Benson followed Claire and Callum into the school. Zane and Zara trailed behind and kept their fans up to date with online updates on their mobile phones.

'Mama,' said Zara, 'this isn't the Talent ...'

Claire quickly interrupted. 'We'll start with the Main Hall. This is where our next big show will be held. It's about the **Titanic** hitting an iceberg and sinking. It's a **disaster** story.'

Callum turned to Claire and whispered: 'Claire, you should stop this right now. We'll get found out.'

Claire waited for the Bensons to walk ahead. 'Don't you see?' she said to Callum. 'All Star High is just like the Titanic. It's the biggest and the best, but there could be a disaster ahead. I'm just trying to stop the disaster before it happens.'

'This idea of yours already is a disaster!' said Callum. But he couldn't let Claire down now. He had to help her out.

21

CHAPTER

They walked to the Main Hall and
Callum explained the show to
Mrs Benson. The stage set was an
enormous wooden model of a ship.

'Our show is not about the

passengers,' said Callum. 'It's about
the band and the music they played.
Today you'll see some of the students
rehearsing.'

He called out to the Gang-Stars who
were getting ready to start their music
rehearsal.

'We're giving the Benson family a
tour. Zane and Zara might want to
come here. Can you show them what
you've been rehearsing?'

The Gang-Stars scrambled into action
and went off stage to get what they
needed.

Jacki already had her violin on the
stage so she stayed behind. 'I'm glad

you're here, Claire,' she said. 'Can you show me how to stand up and balance?'

'But you already are standing up and balancing!' said Zane. 'What's the problem?'

'The problem is that it's hard to stand up and balance when the ship starts rocking,' said Claire. 'Come with me and see.'

Zane and Zara were interested now.

'Make the ship start rocking,' said Zane.

'No,' said Claire. 'It has to be tested first. We don't know if it's safe yet.'

Zane and Zara were not used to

being told 'No'. They always got what they wanted. What they wanted now was to be on a ship that could rock. They could film it all and put it on their web page so their fans would see.

Claire showed the twins the backstage area and the dressing room. As they walked back into the Main Hall Zara and Zane hung back.

'When they've all gone we'll switch the ship on,' said Zane.

'You can sing and I'll dance while it rocks,' said Zara. 'We can **live stream** it to our website.

'I'll put a message on the website now so our fans keep watching,' said Zane.

'Great,' said Zara. 'We haven't been in the news for days. Our fans and the **reporters** should be here soon.'

Mrs Benson sat down to watch the rehearsal. She put Ginger the dog on her lap. The band started to play while Claire and the other dancers danced. Mrs Benson liked what she heard and saw.

'Bravo,' she cried. She held Ginger's paws and made the dog clap.

Claire and Callum continued the tour with Mrs Benson, Ginger and the twins. The Gang-Stars decided to tag along. Nobody saw the twins turn and head back to the Main Hall.

Zane and Zara went up on stage. They walked around the ship. At the back was a high pressure air pump. Zara plugged one end of the pump to the ship. The other end was plugged in to the **power socket** at the back of the stage.

Zara and Zane both heard noises and turned to look into the hall. A small group of fans and reporters had arrived. It was time to start!

'Quick,' called Zane. 'Switch on the power and get on to the ship!'

Zara switched on the power and they both jumped up on to the rocking ship.

28

CHAPTER

The tour group was in the dance
studio. A boy with spiky red hair turned
cartwheels as he said, 'You need to get
back to the Main Hall,' he said. 'Now!'

As they raced down the corridor,

Claire said, 'Do you know him?'

'No,' said Callum. 'I don't think so.'

Callum and Claire pushed open the doors and rushed into the Main Hall. They stopped in surprise. The ship was rocking! Had their teacher Miss Spark arrived and turned on the power? No! Zane or Zara must have done it. They were on the ship, singing and dancing, while the twins' fans and some reporters filmed them.

Callum and Claire ran down the aisle and up on to the stage. Callum was about to turn off the power and tell off the twins. He didn't.

'What should we do?' he asked

Claire in a whisper.

Claire wasn't sure. The rocking ship wasn't a problem for anyone else.

'Nothing, I guess,' she said. 'They'll be finished soon.'

Mrs Benson went up on to the stage. 'My darlings,' she cried. 'You look amazing. Ginger and I are coming on board.'

The twins looked horrified. They had their fans and the reporters here. No way did they want to be filmed with their mother.

Just as Mrs Benson walked on to the ship it jerked to the left. Then it jerked to the right. The ship started to shake and rock. Zane and Zara lost their balance and fell to the floor. Mrs Benson lost her balance too. Ginger leapt out of her arms and ran into the ship.

Callum and Claire quickly turned off the power and the ship stopped moving.

'This will make All Star High look really bad,' said Callum. 'Now no students will want to come here.'

'What else can go wrong?' moaned Claire.

Zane and Zara jumped to their feet.

'That *rocked*!' said Zane. 'Did you guys film all that?

Mrs Benson suddenly cried out. 'Ginger!'

Callum and Claire ran over to Mrs Benson.

'What's the matter?' asked Claire.

'Ginger's stuck inside the ship!' said Mrs Benson.

'GINGER,' shouted Callum. 'Here, boy.'

'Girl,' corrected Mrs Benson. 'But my baby can't hear you – she's deaf. Ginger's also blind, she won't be able to get out on her own.'

Callum and Claire looked into the ship. They could see a gap in the floorboard of the deck. It was big enough for a small dog to fall down into the wooden frame below the ship.

'It needs someone small but strong to drag the dog out,' said Callum.

Mrs Benson dabbed at her eyes. 'Thank you,' she said.

Callum shook his head. 'Not me. I'm too big. Claire is smaller. She'll rescue Ginger.'

'Umm, maybe ... I'm not sure I can do it,' said Claire. 'There's not much room to move down there.'

'With your ballet training, you're really **flexible**,' said Callum. 'You'll easily get through. I'll go to the side of the ship and try to see or hear Ginger.'

Soon he called, 'I can hear her. She's over this side.'

Claire squeezed down through the gap until she was under the floorboard of the ship's deck. She hated being in small, dark places. Her heart was thumping and it was hard to breathe because of all the dust. The wooden frame of the ship made it hard to move.

'I can't do this', she thought. 'I'm going back'. Then she heard a sad whimper. It was Ginger. Claire knew she had to go on.

36

CHAPTER

'It's all right, Ginger. I'm coming,' Claire called out.

'The dog's deaf,' Callum reminded her. 'She can't hear you. Can you see her yet? She's over this side, near me.'

'I can't see. It's too dark,' called Claire. 'I don't think I can do this.'

Callum could hear that Claire was starting to panic. 'Keep calm and listen to me,' he called. 'I'm going to sing, and you just need to keep coming towards my voice. Just concentrate on the song and don't think about anything else. You can do it, Claire.'

Callum start to sing. His singing did two things. First, it helped Claire to know which way to go. Second, it helped her to calm down. She wasn't as worried about being in the small dark place any more. She just concentrated on the singing.

Claire heard the sad whimper again. It was closer this time.

'I can see Ginger. You can stop singing now,' she said.

When Ginger smelled Claire she trotted up to her and licked her face. Claire crawled backwards to the gap with Ginger following her. Then she passed Ginger up through the gap to Mrs Benson.

'*Bravo*, Claire,' she said. 'That was very brave of you to rescue Ginger.'

'Now we need to get you out, too,' said Callum. He reached down, grabbed Claire's hands and carefully pulled her out of the gap.

'Great job, Claire,' he said.

Claire blinked as video cameras were pushed in her face.

'Tell us about the rescue,' one voice said.

'What was it like?' asked another.

The reporters had Ginger's adventure on film.

'Everyone loves a trapped pet story,' said one reporter. 'Plus we have a famous family and a rescue. This will be on the news tonight for sure.'

'Hey,' said Zane. 'What about us? Me and Zara are the story, not Ginger.'

But the reporters weren't interested in Zane and Zara. They were filming

Mrs Benson and the rescued dog.

'Claire and Callum are amazing students,' said Mrs Benson. 'They've really learned how to perform under **pressure**.' She turned and looked into the camera. 'So I want everyone to know that this school ...' Mrs Benson paused.

Claire turned to Callum.

'Oh no,' she said. 'She's going to say the Talent Academy.'

'This school ... All Star High, will give you the best training you could ever want,' said Mrs Benson. 'Not just training in performing arts, but training for real life, too.'

This time it was Callum's turn to nudge Claire. 'I think you've just done *two* superhero rescues!' he said. 'You've saved Ginger *and* All Star High! Not such a disaster after all!'

GLOSSARY

autograph – when someone famous signs their name for a fan

bravo – an Italian word that people call out at a show, meaning 'Well done!'

disaster – something that has gone terribly wrong

entertainment – something to watch and enjoy

flexible – able to bend easily

live stream – show something online as it happens

open day – a day for people to visit a school or company to see what it is like

performing arts – all kinds of performance: acting, singing, dancing and music

power socket – where you can plug in electrical things

pressure – a difficult situation

reality show – a TV programme showing people's real lives

rehearsal – practising a show or a performance

reporter – someone who gets the news and pictures for TV programmes or newspapers

stretch limousine – a very long car often used by celebrities; can be called a 'limo' for short

Titanic – a big strong ship which unexpectedly sank on its first trip in 1912

QUIZ

1 Which Gang-Star did Callum see standing at the school gate?

2 What is the name of the new school?

3 What kind of stage did the new school have?

4 Why did the flier have All Star High's address on it?

5 Why were Zane and Zara Benson famous?

6 Who was Ginger?

7 What does 'bravo' mean?

8 Why couldn't the dog hear Claire calling to it?

9 In what two ways did Callum's singing help Claire?

10 How did Ginger know when Claire got close?

ANSWERS

1 Claire Stevens

2 The Talent Academy

3 A revolving stage.

4 There must have been a printing error.

5 They had won a reality TV show called *Who's Going to be a Star?*.

6 Mrs Benson's small dog.

7 'Well done'

8 The dog was deaf.

9 It showed her which way to go, and it calmed her down.

10 It could smell her.

ABOUT THE AUTHOR

Helen Chapman is an Australian author of eighty books who has been published in the United Kingdom, the U.S.A, New Zealand and Australia. She has travelled extensively and lived in America and England and is currently living in Australia.

For further information on Helen and her books visit: www.helenchapman.com

Helen has a special friend Rose Inserra who knows what her contribution has been to the ASH series and who can never be sufficiently thanked for it.

The All Star High books are available from most
booksellers. For more information or to order,
please call Rising Stars on 0800 091 1602 or visit
www.risingstars-uk.com

RISING ★ STARS

head in the twenties style, forming a cap which
d in two small semi-circles to frame the cheekbones.
a Suffolk Shore', the only painting which, to his
Quinn had admitted owning in his letter to Gifford,
sable from its subject matter: a woman lying naked
-dunes, a man, also nude, standing beside her.
st canvas, which Finch left to the last, was the
ilith for which Quinn had given Zoe Hamilton five
ash. There was no mistaking the fact that it made a
one hanging in Max Gifford's bedroom. As in that
man's face was hidden but the body had the same
and cascade of dark, flowing hair.
a sudden desire to touch it, he leaned forward and
f one finger over the canvas. It seemed to come alive
uch as he felt the texture of the paint, rough and
ere the marks of brush and palette knife were
he pigment, a mute and static token of the passion
hey had first been applied.
tin was still typing out the list when he returned to
d, when she had completed it and handed it to him,
quickly down it. She hadn't been exaggerating;
over forty names on it, together with addresses,
umbers and the dates on which Quinn had been in
each individual. Alongside some of them, she had
n their business or personal status where it was
ier – accountant, bank manager, fellow club-
me were not listed in this manner and Finch
t, in these cases, she had no record of their exact
with Quinn. Only one of the names rang a bell in
at of Bruce Lawford, which seemed faintly familiar
ich could not remember where he had heard it. Or
it, for he associated it vaguely with the printed
ly a newspaper report he had read, the details of
d now forgotten. There was no indication of what
ord did for a living or why Quinn should have had
im; which, according to the date, he had done on
th, St Valentine's Day, Finch realised, another

headmistress's quiet speculation, as if running an eye over him
with the intention of writing some comment at the end of his
school report.

Finch admitted that Quinn's murder was indeed the purpose
of his visit and hurried into his next remark before she had time
to assume control of the interview which, given half a chance,
she would do.

'I understand Mr Quinn was thinking of mounting an
exhibition of Max Gifford's work.'

'That's right. Why do you ask? Does it have any bearing on
Mr Quinn's death?' she demanded as if he were under inter-
rogation.

'If you'd just answer my question,' Finch replied pleasantly.

He won the round but not without one of those ridiculous
confrontations in which they stared at each other in silence for
several seconds before Miss Martin conceded defeat, which she
signalled by removing her spectacles – without which her face
looked naked and much more vulnerable.

'He discussed it with me, of course. He'd arranged to see Mr
Gifford on Thursday and I entered the meeting in his appointments book. I also left Friday free as well as I understood there
was an auction in the same area which he wanted to attend. The
two dates coincided quite satisfactorily.'

But not entirely coincidentally, as Blanche Lester had made
clear.

'When he discussed the exhibition with you, was any date
mentioned?'

'No, although Mr Quinn said that if the meeting with Mr
Gifford went as well as he hoped, he'd aim for a date in late
spring next year.'

Which corroborated Max Gifford's statement, Finch
thought, and also brought him to the main purpose of the
interview.

'Did he mention a business partner?'

Her response was immediate.

'What partner? Mr Quinn has no partner. The gallery is
owned, or rather leased, in Mr Quinn's name only. As far as I

am aware, he never considered taking anyone else into the business.'

'He spoke of a partner to Max Gifford; someone who was going to help finance the exhibition.'

'But Mr Quinn had no need to ask for outside financial backing. The gallery is perfectly able to cover the costs of any exhibition we might choose to mount.'

She seemed to be taking it personally, as if any suggestion of financial dependence on outsiders somehow reflected on her own efficiency. Judging by his surroundings, Finch could well believe her denial. Quinn hadn't been short of money. Why then the talk of a partner? And why only to Max Gifford and not to his own secretary, who appeared to know about all other aspects of his business affairs?

'Perhaps Miss Lester could help you,' Miss Martin continued. 'Have you asked her? She may be more intimate with Mr Quinn's arrangements.'

The significance of the word occurred to her too late and Finch saw her colour rise. For a moment she looked uncharacteristically flustered, and Finch wondered what she thought of the relationship between Quinn and Blanche Lester. No doubt she disapproved. She might even feel a little resentful.

'I have asked her,' he replied, pretending not to have noticed her momentary confusion. 'Miss Lester knows nothing about it either.'

'Then I'm afraid I can't help you,' she stated flatly.

'There is one thing you can do for me. You spoke of Mr Quinn's appointments book. I'd like a list of the names and addresses of all the people he had any contact with since January.'

He chose the date deliberately because, according to Askew, this was about the time when Quinn had bought the first of Max Gifford's sketches and was the earliest date, he calculated, that the idea of acquiring more of Gifford's work and of mounting the exhibition must have occurred to him.

'All of them?' Miss Martin protested. 'But there must be dozens!'

'I'd like the list all the same,' Finch [...] you're preparing it, perhaps I could [...] paintings by Max Gifford which Mr Q[...] they're kept in the gallery?'

'They're downstairs in the baseme[...] way.'

Miss Martin rose to her feet and [...] passage, from which a flight of steps led [...] protected by a heavy steel door whi[...] swinging it open and switching on [...] storage space beyond.

It was large, extending under both t[...] and was lined with vertical metal racks [...] ceiling, in which canvases of all size[...] curtains of white sheeting. The faint [...] the freshness of the atmosphere sugg[...] air-conditioning was in operation. A s[...] along the ceiling cast a hard, white, al[...]

Miss Martin appeared to know exac[...] was stored, for she went without hesita[...] and drew out seven canvases, the las[...] help her lift forward and lean against [...]

'I'll leave you to examine them whil[...] him. 'When you've finished, I'll put th[...] up.'

Not trusting him evidently even [...] waited until she had departed befor[...] the paintings. They were propped u[...] of the pictures he had seen ranged i[...] Gifford's dining-room and, remem[...] difficulty in recognising Gifford's s[...] were portraits, mostly of women, on[...] Zoe Hamilton when young, standin[...] and admiring, with the same expre[...] tion he had seen on her face in the p[...] body; but, in all other respects, h[...] youthful, the breasts high and poin[...]

close [...]
curled [...]

'Fig[...]
knowl[...]
was re[...]
among[...]

The [...]
portra[...]
hundre[...]
pair wi[...]
one, th[...]
fluid b[...]

Mov[...]
ran the [...]
under [...]
sensual[...]
petrifie[...]
with w[...]

Miss [...]
the offic[...]
he glan[...]
there w[...]
telepho[...]
contact [...]
also typ[...]
known [...]
member[...]
assumed [...]
relations[...]
his mind,[...]
although [...]
rather, re[...]
word; pos[...]
which he [...]
Bruce Law[...]
lunch with[...]
February [...]

familiar detail which fixed both the time and the name in his mind.

Pocketing the sheet of paper, he thanked her before adding casually, 'By the way, what would a portrait by a modern painter fetch these days?'

'It depends who the artist is,' Miss Martin replied in a voice that was intended to put him in his place for displaying such ignorance. 'If you're talking of Picasso, then you're in the several hundred thousand pound bracket, perhaps even a quarter of a million or more. Work by a less well-known but collectable artist, an Augustus John for example, might fetch anything up to twenty thousand. But those figures are only approximate. There are so many other factors to take into consideration, the quality of the painting, for example, or the competition to buy. Picasso or Matisse are still much sought after, of course; Augustus John less so than he was, although his sister, Gwen John, is now highly desirable.'

An interesting point, Finch thought, as he left the office. So it was possible that, working on a conservative estimate of £5,000 a painting, Quinn could have made a profit of £30,000 or more from the seven Gifford paintings he had in his possession, assuming the exhibition had established Gifford's reputation; not bad when his initial investment must have been a mere couple of thousand pounds.

Returning along the passage to the gallery, he found Blanche Lester displaying a large oil-painting of a seascape on an easel to three neatly-tailored Japanese businessmen who were standing in a semicircle in front of it, regarding it with unsmiling attention.

They were unaware of his presence and Finch was able to watch from the doorway the little scene that was being enacted. Blanche Lester, in her white dress, looked like a small girl playing at schools, the three men her pupils, standing obediently before her, grouped politely, all with their hands clasped behind their backs as if assuming a regulation pose set down in some manual of etiquette on the correct stance to adopt when viewing a painting.

The painting in question was huge and ornately framed, depicting a stormy sea with a ship in full sail leaning to the wind, and was full of frantic movement – spray flying, clouds racing, flags streaming – immobilised on the canvas and symbolising, for Finch, at least, that very English sea-dog attitude epitomised in such heroes as Drake or Nelson.

Heaven knows what the Japanese businessmen made of it, and he tried to imagine it hanging in one of their elegant, flimsy houses of oiled paper and bamboo; an absurd conception, of course; one of those conditioned images from childhood which would never be entirely superseded, despite television and the cinema, by pictures of present-day Japan with its skyscrapers and modern office-blocks. On the same basis, he would always think of Eskimos in igloos and Red Indians in tepees, so firmly had the illustrations in his primary-school geography book impressed themselves on his imagination.

The group seemed absorbed, but some sixth sense must have warned Blanche Lester of his presence for she glanced in his direction and, having murmured an excuse to her clients, crossed the gallery towards him, the three men all bowing in unison at her departure and following her with their eyes.

'I'm afraid this is going to take longer than I thought. Can you come back later?' she asked in a low voice.

'What time do you close?' Finch inquired.

'Six o'clock.'

He glanced at his watch. It was nearly a quarter past five, time to get himself tea, and he nodded in agreement before turning, on a sudden, inexplicable whim, to bow his apologies to the Japanese whose private view he had interrupted, and who, surprised and gratified by this courtesy, bowed deeply back. As he left, he could feel their ripple of astonishment follow him in almost audible, tinkling waves.

They were gone when he returned and Blanche Lester was alone, in the act of spreading a dust-sheet over the desk. Seeing him through the window, she gestured that she would join him outside and, pausing to turn off the spotlights only and close the door behind her, she came out into the street.

'Is that all?' Finch asked, the policeman in him outraged by her perfunctory preparations for securing the place for the night. 'Don't you have grilles to pull down over the windows?'

'Miss Martin supervises the locking-up,' she explained. 'There's a caretaker who does it but she goes round with him. She holds all the keys, you see.'

It was a piece of information which didn't entirely surprise him, remembering Miss Martin's insistence that she herself would lock up the basement store-room after him. All the same, he wondered a little at the arrangement. Although Blanche Lester had been Eustace Quinn's lover, Quinn evidently hadn't trusted her to the extent of giving her keys to the gallery, an ambivalent situation to find herself in, he would have imagined, although she seemed to accept it.

By common, unspoken consent, they walked towards Piccadilly, crossing over it and entering the park where they turned in the direction of the underground station; her habitual route home, he supposed.

The noise of the traffic made conversation impossible and, even when they reached the comparative peace of the park, Finch seemed in no hurry to begin the interview. Content to remain silent, he strolled along beside her, conscious that she was matching her pace to his and that normally she would have hurried, anxious to catch her train home.

'It's very beautiful here,' he said at last, and indeed it was. Behind the plane trees, their piebald bark reminding him of small, jigsaw pieces of different shades of brown, intricately pieced together, the traffic went roaring up Piccadilly, sounding at that distance like the low growling of some restless animal, while above the trees the pale stones façades of the buildings with their many windows caught the late afternoon sun. But here, in the park, was a very different world to the throngs of people passing to and fro in front of the glittering car showrooms and the international airline offices, although some home-going commuters, hurrying along the paths to the tube station or the bus stops, introduced some of that frenetic activity even here.

Otherwise there was only sky, trees and grass. And lovers. They lay in attitudes of slumber, face to face, oblivious of the passers-by. In the distance, a woman threw a stick for a dog again and again. It was too far away to hear its barking, only its leaping form was apparent, paws and head uplifted in joyful, heraldic gestures.

Blanche Lester did not reply to his remark and he hadn't expected an answer, although he glanced sideways at her as if anticipating one. Her profile was serene but blank, unaware of anything about her, even the admiring glances of the men who, passing her, looked directly into her face, caught by her beauty, and Finch was again reminded of the children's story, first evoked by Zoe Hamilton, which was now projected onto Blanche Lester. Extending the comparison, she could be likened to the Sleeping Beauty herself, the princess from the same fairy story whom the prince awakened with a kiss, a thought which might have been partly induced by the sight of the couples lying in the grass in one another's arms.

But who would awaken her? Certainly not the men who glanced at her as they passed. Nor, apparently, had Eustace Quinn succeeded in arousing her. She seemed as untouched by that affair as if it had never happened.

With this thought in his mind, it seemed quite natural to ask the question which, after all, was the reason for his being there.

'Why did you and Eustace Quinn quarrel on Friday morning?'

Its effect on her was more dramatic than he had foreseen. She stopped abruptly and, turning to face him, forced him also to halt in his tracks. He saw that she was at last awakened.

'Who told you that?' she demanded, her voice imperious. 'Oh, I can guess! Someone at the hotel, I expect; a snooper, listening in to other people's conversations. Does that please you, picking up that sort of tittle-tattle? Do you get job-satisfaction from it?'

'It's certainly part of my work, listening to gossip,' Finch admitted, more mildly than he felt. In fact, he was acutely embarrassed by her outburst and conscious of the stares of the passers-by, amused at the sight of the shabby middle-aged man and the beautiful young girl quarrelling in public, or so it must have seemed to them. A lovers' tiff? their expressions seemed to be asking. Oh, hardly! I mean, he must be years older than her.

As abruptly and unexpectedly, her mood changed.

'Oh, I'm sorry, so sorry!' she cried, like a child close to tears and, partly to comfort her and partly to break up the confrontation, he drew her arm through his where he could feel it trembling against his side.

'You know, you'll have to tell what happened,' he explained, gently avuncular.

With subdued obedience, she replied, 'Of course. I understand you have to know.'

Finch was struck again, as he had been the previous day, by her apparent candour and ingenuousness, which he felt he was at last beginning to understand a little better. It was, or rather had been, a natural part of her personality which, when confronted by Quinn's aggression and deviousness, she had been forced to exaggerate in much the same way as shy people will increase their diffidence in the company of an extrovert. It was a defensive pose, assumed in an attempt to protect her own individuality against the pressure of a stronger and more ruthless character and, once having found its uses, she could no longer return to the guileless innocence of its original form. The artlessness was now touched up by art and the ingenuousness had become self-conscious.

They had begun walking again, still arm in arm, pacing slowly along the path. After a silence, in which he refrained from pressing her for an answer, she started speaking in a hesitant, tentative manner.

'It was about Nina; the quarrel, I mean. Eustace had been flirting with her on Thursday. Oh, please, don't misunderstand me; I didn't really mind. It was the sort of thing he was always doing, only this time it was different. I can't explain it properly, but I felt he was using her, and somehow it all seemed so stupid and so mixed up with everything else; not just Eustace and me but Max and Nina as well. It made me think about couples –

men and women being together, I mean; not about marriage so much as the way they see each other in relation to themselves. It occurred to me on Thursday, for example, when I first met Max and Nina, how incredibly selfish, in fact, Max was. I suppose that sounds an awful thing to say? I mean, he's a marvellous person in so many ways – talented and charming and terribly amusing – but that's *him*. Do you understand? Him, by himself; nothing to do with Nina.'

Finch nodded, encouraging her to continue, although he was not sure where this disjointed account was leading to and thinking, at the same time, that the Max she was describing was nothing like the old, sick man he had interviewed on Friday afternoon after Eustace Quinn's murder.

'The point is,' she continued, 'He's not a different person with Nina; he's still Max; himself; nothing's been altered.'

'Should it be?' Finch asked.

'I'm not sure. It's one of the things I've been trying to decide. I felt he ought to change. Nina does. She's quite different when she's alone to when she's with him. Then she just seems to be Max's woman, as if she switches off most of herself and is absorbed into him. I know he's old now and needs looking after but it's really got nothing to do with that. I feel it's always been the same between them, Max taking and Nina giving, and the worst part is I don't think it's ever occurred to him what's happening or that there might be anything wrong in it.'

'Perhaps Nina accepts the situation,' Finch suggested.

She flashed up again at once, her mood changing so rapidly that Finch wondered if she were not unbalanced in some way; neurotic, possibly, although her behaviour could have been caused by the shock of Quinn's death. All the same, it occurred to him that a girl with hysterical tendencies and what appeared to be a deep-seated resentment against her former lover made a good candidate for a murder suspect. Pushed that little bit too far, she could easily go over the edge into a full-blown neurosis in which there was no guarantee she would act rationally. He could see, however, how this conflict in her personality could have been caused by her own uncertainty about what role she was to assume, child or woman. He was also willing to bet that when Quinn became her lover she had been a virgin, and that he had almost entirely been to blame for the corruption of her innocence, not the mere physical deflowering but the despoliation of her own clear self-image.

'Then she shouldn't accept it,' she cried. 'She ought to set a higher value on herself. Besides, it's so unfair!'

It was the protest a child might have uttered, confronted by the injustice of life and aware that there was nothing to be done about it.

'Max may not see it like that,' Finch pointed out reasonably.

'Of course he doesn't! Why should he? That way he gets the cake *and* the icing.'

'And is that how you saw your relationship with Eustace Quinn?' Finch asked, deftly turning the subject back to its main point.

'Oh, Eustace!' she said disparagingly as if he were still alive. 'Eustace is far worse than Max. At least Max doesn't really know he's doing it.'

'But Eustace does?' Finch prompted, using the present tense as she had done.

'I told you yesterday, he's never done anything without thinking it out first.'

'Like flirting with Nina?'

'He was attracted. He probably really wanted to make love to her. But it was all carefully planned.'

'And that's why you quarrelled?'

'Yes,' she admitted simply. 'How stupid it all seems now he's dead! But it was important at the time. You see, I suddenly realised that I was like Nina; someone to be used in a relationship; never really allowed to be myself. It was the reason why I drove round yesterday morning instead of going straight to the preview as he wanted me to. I thought, Why should I always do exactly what he tells me? Childish, wasn't it? But he always expected me to fit in with his plans. That's why I was taken down to Althorpe in the first place.'

'I don't understand,' Finch told her. He had genuinely lost

the thread of her reasoning and, surprised by his honesty, she looked at him directly, a curious expression lifting the corners of her mouth; hardly a smile, more like a wry twisting of the lips.

'Didn't you know? My job was to pump Nina about herself.'

'Why was that?' Finch asked as casually as he could. Her remark, however, had shaken him. Zoe Hamilton had made almost the same comment concerning Eustace Quinn's interest in Nina Gifford which, at the time, he had dismissed as mere spitefulness. Now, it would appear Quinn had been following a deliberate, planned inquiry.

'I don't know. He just said, "Find out as much as you can about her."'

'And did you?'

'Yes, on Thursday. It didn't occur to me then that there was anything wrong in what I was doing. Nina asked me to walk in the garden after lunch and I got her to talk about herself. It wasn't difficult.'

Again he saw her lips lift and twist with that strangely bitter, ashamed wryness as if there were a faintly unpleasant flavour in her mouth.

'What did she tell you?'

'All about her marriage to Max. She was seventeen when she met him and still at school. She ran away from home to join him in London. To listen to her, you'd've thought she was describing some wonderful romance, the sort of story you read in women's magazines, love at first sight and happy ever after,' she said with the same tone of disparaging mockery with which she had spoken Eustace Quinn's name.

Romance. For some reason the word stuck in Finch's mind, although he couldn't think why. It became mixed up with other images: Alice in Wonderland and the fairy-story princess, tales from his childhood and the sweet innocence of their illustrations which, in turn, were overlaid by the more recent images of Zoe's and Lilith's naked bodies seen through Max Gifford's eyes.

Suddenly, without any warning and taking him totally by surprise, his thoughts occupied elsewhere, Blanche Lester began running, her white dress and black hair streaming out behind her like a maenad's as she fled towards the ramped path which led up to the entrance to the underground station. Finch set off in pursuit but, after a short distance, abandoned the idea. It was hopeless attempting to catch up with her. The last glimpse he caught of her before she disappeared into the home-going crowds was the pale flicker of her dress against the railings.

Well, it couldn't be helped. If necessary he could always interview her again, although he suspected she had told him all she knew and that her sudden flight had been caused not so much by a desire to escape from him and his questions but from herself.

He strolled towards the exit, taking his time. Tomorrow was Sunday, so there was no chance of interviewing any of the people on Miss Martin's list; not even Bruce Lawford whose name, with its maddening but unidentified familiarity, occurred to him again. Never mind. On Monday, he'd get Boyce and Kyle, possibly Marsh as well, to come up to town and see each individual in turn. That way the man's identity ought to be discovered. He'd also ask Boyce to set in motion an inquiry into Nina Gifford's past for, as he'd already be in London, the sergeant could start at the Records Office on a simple check of a few basic facts about her, such as the exact date of Max Gifford's divorce from Zoe Hamilton and his subsequent marriage to her.

As for himself, he'd drop in at Althorpe House, making the visit look casual, and show her Max's sketches in order to see just what her reaction would be. With any luck, he might even get to the bottom of her relationship with Danny Webb at the same time.

Which reminded him that, while he was in London, there was one more move he could make regarding Danny Webb and that was to call in at Scotland Yard and check if Webb had a police record, a possibility which had first occurred to him when he had seen him and Nina together in the yard at Althorpe House but which would need verification before he confronted both Danny and Nina with a few uncomfortable facts about themselves and the murder of Eustace Quinn.

I I

Danny woke early, aware that it was Sunday morning; a hangover from childhood, he decided. There had been a special quality then about Sunday mornings, an extra, anticipatory hush about the house as if its atmosphere had thickened and grown more dense during the night. He could always sense it even before the bells began ringing for Communion.

This morning there were no bells; it was too early. All the same, reaching up to pull aside one of the little curtains over the caravan window above the bed, he saw the garden was holding itself motionless with that familiar, awed expectancy.

It was half past six, he realised, checking his watch.

Shit! He had meant to be off before there was any chance of Lionel being awake. He was usually up and about by seven, a routine which probably extended into the weekend as well. Lionel was a man of regular habits. He had been out cutting the bloody lawn at quarter to eight one morning, on purpose, Danny suspected, to put to shame his own preference for a lie-in until the pub was open.

Flinging aside the bedclothes, he dressed hurriedly and then began collecting up his scattered possessions, stuffing them into a suitcase and snapping it shut. There was not even bloody time to shave or make coffee.

At the door he paused and then, smiling to himself, tramped back across the bed, deliberately grinding his feet into the sheets, and switched on the boiling ring anyway. With any luck it would be hours before Lionel discovered it had been left burning.

Outside, he eyed the back of the cottage speculatively. The bedroom curtains were still drawn, which probably meant Lionel wasn't yet up, though Danny wasn't prepared to risk it.

To reach the road, he'd have to crunch his way along the shingled drive. Better to make off across the fields, he decided. He could get to Nina's through the shrubbery gate and sit it out in the summer-house until he could contact her. He might even shove a note through the letter-box telling her where he was so that he wouldn't be kept hanging about for too long. He was down to his last three cigarettes and he didn't relish having to wait without fags indefinitely.

In the event, he couldn't send the note. He had no bloody pen or pencil on him, he discovered when he reached the summer-house. Going through his pockets, he laid the contents out on the bench. Cigarette packet and lighter – the one he'd nicked from the bar of the Feathers; well, people ought to take more care of their belongings – the key to his room at the Dolphin which he hadn't bothered to return, a crumpled handkerchief, a letter from some woman in Clapham and two pounds and forty-nine pence.

He tore the letter into pieces, carrying them outside in the cupped palms of his hands before tossing them into the air to let the upward draught carry them away; little, white scraps of paper which fluttered for a few moments and then sank to the damp grass like broken-winged butterflies. The money he doled out along the wooden slats of the bench-seat, weighing the notes down with the key and piling up the silver and copper coins into two little stacks. But no fucking pen. Flinging himself back against the rough timber wall, he folded his arms moodily and settled down to wait.

Nina got up at eight o'clock, her thoughts on Danny, though she was unaware of his proximity. After all, she hadn't been able, as she had intended, to see him on Friday after Finch had left. That evening, Max had claimed all her attention, calling her upstairs on various pretexts, like a child who, unable to sleep, doesn't see why the grown-ups shouldn't be equally discommoded. By the time she had finally settled him down, it was too late to set off for Lionel's and, besides, she had felt too tired to make the effort.

She had called instead on Saturday morning, telling Max that she was going to the village shop, but Danny had been out. Lionel had met her in the garden, bustling out of the house to waylay her the moment she turned the corner, but with none of his usual signs of pleasure. In fact, he had been quite cool and off-hand towards her; probably the memory of that stupid business between herself and Eustace Quinn still rankled even though Quinn was now dead; or he was annoyed with Danny and was punishing him through her, an interpretation that seemed justified by the air of quiet triumph with which Lionel announced that Danny was out and he, Lionel, had no idea when he would be back.

As far as he was concerned, the later the better, his tone implied.

Oh, sod you, then, Nina had thought, cycling home. Who cares anyway?

But she was more distressed than she had at first cared to admit. Lionel's defection was added to her general disquiet, augmenting it and at the same time distracting it towards yet another source of worry without diminishing its other causes: Eustace Quinn's murder, of course, and Max, but mainly Danny.

Danny was up to something. Nina had been aware of that as she had talked to him in the yard on Friday. Trouble had been written all over him. In a confused way, she had tried to get to the bottom of it but, exhausted mentally and psychologically by the events of the past few days, she had been unable to think it through properly or put her finger on its exact cause. Danny had been uneasy and tense, that much was certain, and the reason wasn't difficult to find: it had been Finch's presence. Which was perfectly understandable. She had long ago realised that Danny had probably got on the wrong side of the law at some stage in his life and, besides, he had always, even as a young child, resented authority of any kind. So when it came down to it, she was worrying unnecessarily, she told herself.

All the same, her fears had been only partially quietened and she had brooded for the rest of the day, although she had made no further attempt to get in touch with Danny. It would only give Lionel another opportunity for showing his disapproval and she was damned if she was going to allow him that satisfaction.

In his turn, Lionel thought of Nina, as he did most of the time, her presence so real in his mind on occasion that, opening a door or turning a corner, he was surprised not to find her actually there. She seemed to overflow her own immediate environment into his, taking up residence in a manner so pervasive that even the most ordinary, everyday objects seemed to be impregnated with her aura.

His Sunday breakfast egg was a trivial and slightly ridiculous example. Cracking it delicately on the rim of the frying-pan before sliding it into the hot fat, Lionel remembered whisking up eggs for Nina on Friday, the day Eustace Quinn's body was discovered, and how, as he stood at the table, she had brushed past him on her way to the sink. Her arms, too, were the colour of the shell, brown and faintly speckled, with the same light sheen polishing the porous surface.

It is all quite absurd! he thought, transferring the egg to his plate and laying it down gently in the centre between the crisply-curled slices of bacon and the two halves of grilled tomato. The egg seemed to stare back at him, a round, yellow eye into which he dug his fork with sudden savagery.

I am obsessed by her. And then, It's got to stop.

It was no use telling himself that he must keep aloof from her. He had tried that yesterday in an attempt to distance her but, misunderstanding his reasons, she had been hurt and finally angry, leaving him with a careless, I-don't-give-a-damn fling of her shoulders, dismissive and contemptuous. She hadn't been near the cottage since, not even to call on Danny, an omission for which Lionel was profoundly grateful. He really didn't want to see either of them again; certainly not Danny; the sooner he left the better. Nina, too, although her absence would be a bereavement as well as a relief.

A lot of the trouble was, he admitted, carrying his plate over to the sink where he left it to soak in hot water, bacon and eggs stains being a nuisance to remove once they had gone cold, that he no longer trusted her. She had come down to earth with a wallop in his estimation; no less desirable but a lot less admirable. Her deviousness distressed him.

Danny was no good. Surely Nina could see that? Whatever their relationship was, and Lionel was beginning to doubt he was the family friend that Nina pretended, Danny's true character must be obvious to her. Absolutely No Good. To emphasise the words, Lionel sent three little jets of washing-up liquid squirting into the bowl of hot, clean water before unbuttoning his cuffs and folding back his shirt-sleeves.

As for Eustace Quinn . . . And here Lionel rested his hands on the bottom of the bowl and stared bleakly out through the window over the sink, remembering with a deep sense of shame that brief glimpse through another kitchen window when he had witnessed them standing together in such close intimacy; shame for his own sake at finding himself in the role of Peeping Tom but shame mostly for her.

She had been sexually aroused. Lionel had been perfectly well aware of that. There had been a strange, glistening quality about her eyes and mouth and her body had been soft and slack as if ready to yield itself to Eustace Quinn's embrace.

The memory dirtied his own fantasies about her; vague dreams of lying with Nina in his arms, never clearly imagined because that would presuppose Max's death and Lionel did not wish for that. But there had been many nights when, half-waking, half-sleeping, he had turned in bed to imagine Nina beside him and had sought for her mouth in the darkness.

Quinn's death had done nothing to erase the memory of Nina's betrayal, not just of Max, although that was bad enough, but of his own longings for her.

About the same time, Nina carried Max's breakfast tray upstairs. Like Danny, she had never cared for Sundays, though her memories were of going to church twice during the day and the aching boredom of sitting on a hard, polished pew or kneeling on a hassock which appeared to be stuffed with sawdust. Aunt Connie had insisted on her wearing hat, gloves and stockings even in the hottest weather.

'You behave and dress like a hoyden for the rest of the week,' she used to say. 'At least look like a lady on Sundays.'

As if God cared! Nina had imagined him, lolling somewhere above their heads, elbow resting on a cloud, as he looked down on them sardonically, amused by her own po-shaped velour hat and Aunt Connie's black felt one skewered viciously to her head with a long pin, and wincing as their voices wavered uncertainly upwards, slightly out of tempo with the asthmatic organ pumping along half a beat behind.

'O worship the King, All-glorious above!'

It had seemed to Nina that God would much prefer them to fling off all their clothes and dance joyously round the church. He would want them to be happy, not stiff and unforgiving like Aunt Connie or serious like father, climbing up into the pulpit and peering at them over the rims of his spectacles with an expression of sad, tried patience as they coughed and rustled before settling down to listen to his sermon.

Nina hadn't given God much thought for years but Sundays still bore a special quality for her. In the old days, when she and Max lived in London, they had always gone out somewhere different on a Sunday, either to the country or to some pub in an unexplored part of the city, Wapping or Ealing or Crouch End, where she had been noisier than usual, laughing and talking too much because the Sabbath streets had reminded her of home. Max had never guessed the reason, though she had seen him looking at her curiously at times, amused by her animation.

Today, it was like a real Sunday, quiet, subdued, with nothing much to look forward to. She hadn't the energy to sparkle and Max was equally apathetic. It seemed as if he had suddenly grown old, the process of senescence accelerated like one of those speeded-up films so that she could almost witness the decay taking place before her eyes. He no longer had the interest even to maintain his old, maddening pretences. Entering his bedroom, she saw he was lying awake, his hands resting listlessly on top of the bedclothes, his eyes open and staring at the opposite wall.

Overwhelmed by his sadness, which seemed to surround him like a palisade through which she could no longer penetrate, and conscious of how alone, in fact, she was, she thought of all those huge, empty rooms stretching out beneath her with no one to keep her company. It was a foretaste of what it would be like when he was dead, although she couldn't express it in so many words. She just thought of it as 'when Max is gone'.

Longing suddenly for his company, she said coaxingly, 'Come downstairs this morning, Max. You could sit in the garden. Look, it's lovely out!'

Going over to the window, she flung out an arm, introducing him, as if for the first time, to the view: the clear, early sunlight reflecting glassily on leaves and blades of grass, the soaring blue sky, very far away this morning, a bowl of pale, fragile porcelain.

Max stopped chewing and, bending his head, looked at her from under his eyebrows with the same sad, peering intensity with which her father had surveyed his congregation, and she couldn't bear it. Letting her arm drop, she turned away.

'No, I don't think I'll bother,' he replied. 'I'm better off in bed. And I don't want any more of this breakfast. Why do you always make the fried bread so bloody hard? It's like eating charcoal.'

There was a petulance in his voice and she took the tray without comment, noticing with a little surge of anger that he had nevertheless managed to spoil all the food on his plate. Everything would have to be thrown away, for she didn't fancy eating his left-overs; odd, she thought, when she considered the other things she did for him without the slightest sense of revulsion.

Later, when she had got him washed and settled down again

in bed, she carried the plate into the kitchen and, as she scraped the food into the bin, her exasperation returned.

All that waste! she thought furiously. But then, *he* doesn't have to worry about making ends meet.

If only something wonderful would happen!

At that exact moment, as if in answer to her wish, a car turned into the yard and she saw, with a sense of foreboding, Finch in his old, crumpled macintosh clamber out of the driving seat and approach the house.

Danny saw the car, too. He had come to the edge of the lawn on several occasions to survey the house but each time the curtains at the upstairs window facing him had been drawn. Although he wasn't sure whose bedroom it was, Nina's or Max's, it was obvious that it was still too early to risk going up to the house and trying to attract Nina's attention. Retreating to the summer-house, he had prepared himself for a longer wait. If only she'd bloody hurry up! he thought. He was down to his last cigarette, which he took several times out of the packet before reluctantly returning it.

On the last occasion, the curtains had been open and he saw Nina at the window, talking to someone inside the room; Max, he assumed. She was standing in half-profile, looking back over her shoulder, one arm extended, but she had turned away and was gone before he could attract her attention. At least, he now knew that she was up. Give her quarter of an hour, he decided, and he'd stroll round to the back of the house where he'd probably find her in the kitchen.

While he waited, he smoked his last cigarette, pitching the stub out onto the grass where it lay smouldering, a thin line of smoke going straight up into the windless air.

The sight of the car in the yard stopped him in his tracks just as he reached the corner and he backed away hurriedly, checking the façade of the house to make sure no one had seen him. This side, thank God, appeared uninhabited. On the ground floor, a series of heavily-barred windows, some of them with frosted glass in their lower panes, suggested little-used pantries and store-rooms. The windows above were blank.

Christ! What the hell do I do now? he thought furiously. He didn't dare hang about. Although the arrival of the car might be perfectly harmless, a Sunday visitor calling on Nina, he couldn't guarantee it. Nor could he be sure that more vehicles might not arrive at any moment, bringing back the police to resume their search of the grounds.

Get out while the going's good, he told himself. It had been bad enough coming face to face with that Inspector, Finch or whatever his name was, on Friday. Since then they'd had another whole day in which to turn up God knows what evidence.

Turning away from the yard, he walked rapidly across the lawn, keeping well out of sight of the house and, crossing an overgrown vegetable garden, he found a gap in the hedge through which he squeezed before setting off across the fields.

The back door was open and Finch knocked at it briefly before entering the kitchen which, he noticed, had reverted to its normal state of untidiness, the various packets and pieces of cooking equipment which Lionel Burnett had so painstakingly put away on Friday again littering the table and work-tops.

Nina Gifford, too, looked more unkempt. She was dressed in an old denim skirt, gone baggy at the knees and backside, the gingham blouse, which he remembered her wearing on Friday, hanging loose outside it, its neck open and the sleeves rolled up to reveal the firm, brown flesh of her throat and arms. He was struck again by her physical magnificence, the wealth of dark red hair, bundled back anyhow but possessing its own life and vigour. He could see why Eustace Quinn had been attracted; possibly Lionel Burnett as well, although Finch hadn't yet had the chance to inquire into that relationship.

How many other men had been drawn to her? Finch wondered. Perhaps this was the secret that Blanche Lester was meant to discover. Although she had spoken of Nina as 'Max's woman', it did not necessarily imply that the Giffords' marriage had been exclusive. But so far, Finch hadn't been able to establish exactly why Quinn had been so interested in Nina's past.

Was it blackmail? Looking round the shabby kitchen, it was difficult to believe that this had been his motive. But perhaps his reasoning had been more subtle. Judging by the evidence that Finch had so far uncovered, Quinn had intended making himself a sizeable profit from Max Gifford's exhibition. Supposing he had planned to use Nina's influence over Max to persuade him to sell the pictures still in his possession at a deflated price or to accept a lower percentage on the sale of them?

That made better sense, he thought. Nina, then, under Quinn's threat of revealing something about her past that she didn't want Max to know about, might have killed him rather than submit to his pressure. He had already proved she could have had the opportunity. That line of reasoning would give her a motive as well.

'What do you want?' Nina asked. She was still standing by the waste-bin, holding Max's plate, and, with a gesture of impatience, she rattled it down on the draining-board among yesterday's unwashed supper-things. In the few moments in which Finch had got out of the car and entered the house, she had regained some of her composure. He was alone, which seemed to suggest it wasn't an official visit, and that in itself was a relief, a lowering of tension which allowed her anxiety to turn to anger, the exasperation she had felt towards Max projecting itself against the stocky, round-shouldered figure of the Chief Inspector, who came ambling into her kitchen as if he were one of the family.

The bloody nerve of it!

'Sorry to bother you on a Sunday but I was passing and I thought I'd drop in,' Finch explained, his excuse ready. 'How's Max?'

'A bit better but I don't want you worrying him,' Nina retorted, springing immediately to Max's defence.

Oh, yes, Finch thought, she'd be quite capable of clobbering someone if she lost her temper. There was fire there all right. And the physical strength as well.

'I don't intend to,' he assured her, smiling and indicating a chair as much as to say, Do you mind if I sit down? – an unspoken appeal to which Nina acquiesced grudgingly. But I'm damned if I'm going to offer him tea, she added to herself.

Once seated at the table, Finch seemed to settle himself down for a chat, nodding towards the window and commenting on the weather, at the same time feeling slowly through the pockets of his raincoat as if looking for some mislaid but not very important object. When he finally found it and laid it on the table in front of him, it turned out to be nothing more than a plain, square, manilla envelope.

As he opened it, he continued in the same gossipy style, 'By the way, we found these in Mr Quinn's briefcase. I wonder if you could help me identify them.'

The casualness of the remark left Nina totally unprepared for the sudden appearance of the sketches which she had given to Danny and which Finch now placed on the table before her among the homely muddle of trivial, domestic objects: the bowl of sugar, a jar of coffee granules and Max's empty tray still scattered with his breakfast crumbs.

She stared down at the top drawing, a sketch of Lilith, aware that her colour was rising and that her silence had stretched beyond normal hesitation.

'They're Max's,' she said at last. What else could she say? She couldn't deny knowledge of that obvious fact.

'Do you know how Eustace Quinn might have got hold of them?'

'I've no idea,' she replied, too quickly this time and, feeling this was inadequate, continued, 'Perhaps Max gave them to him. Or he took them without asking.'

She added the rider deliberately, aware of the pitfalls her first explanation led her into. Finch might insist on questioning Max which would, of course, reveal that he knew nothing about them. At least, there was no way Finch could check on Eustace Quinn's actions.

To her relief, Finch appeared satisfied with this response for, gathering up the sketches, he returned them to the envelope which he replaced in his pocket. His expression as he got to his feet was bland, giving nothing away.

'That's all, then, Mrs Gifford, for the moment,' he remarked pleasantly. 'I'm sorry I had to call on a Sunday. I'll leave you in peace now.'

Peace! Nina thought as she watched his car reverse and drive out of the yard. Now he had gone, she had the opportunity to consider more carefully the implications behind his visit. Danny and Eustace Quinn were connected in some way. That much was obvious. If Finch had found the sketches in Eustace Quinn's possession, then it could only mean that, directly or indirectly, he had acquired them from Danny. And once that link was made, it opened up all kinds of other terrifying possibilities which she hardly dared think about rationally and which only expressed themselves in sudden, quick fears, darting through her mind like the shadows of fish seen at the bottom of a dark pond.

First there was Danny's anxiety and tension on Friday; in fact, the whole reason behind his visit, for she no longer believed that he had come to the house on her account. Then his absence from the caravan on Friday morning when she had gone to Lionel's to telephone the police after discovering Eustace Quinn's body. Added to this was Danny's chronic shortage of money, his leaving London, her feeling that he was in some kind of trouble . . .

Oh, God! There seemed no end to it. But out of all the confusion one thought stood out clearly. She'd have to warn him. So far, it seemed unlikely that Finch knew how Eustace Quinn had got hold of the drawings but he might not remain in ignorance for long. She must get to Danny before he did.

Running into the hall, intending to call up the stairs to Max, she changed her mind. He would only delay her and, with a little luck, she'd be back before he missed her. Instead, she fetched her bike from the stable and, without even stopping to close the back door behind her, she cycled off down the drive.

While the interview with Nina was still proceeding, Lionel came out of the cottage, carrying a full watering-can which he held awkwardly away from himself so that it wouldn't come into contact with the trousers of his best suit. He was dressed for church but, since changing his clothes, he had noticed the fuchsias were flagging in their pots and had decided to water them. Later, the sun would be on them and to do so then would risk causing leaf-scorch.

Tipping the can carefully so as not to swamp them, he watched the water soak down into the soil and imagined, with a small, wry smile at his own fanciful extravagance, that he could hear the little, fibrous roots sucking it in. From them, it would be siphoned upwards, circulating gently like clear plasma through the complex, upright tubes of the stems and into the narrow veins in the leaves. Squatting down beside the last tub, he fondled one of the shoots gently, feeling the thin, green flesh cool under his finger-tips.

As he straightened up he glanced towards the end of the garden, wondering if Danny was awake yet, and noticed the half-drawn curtain, although its significance did not strike him particularly. What caught his attention was the sun shining on some broken glass at the foot of the steps where a beer bottle, rolling off the top of the box crammed with empties, had smashed on the flagstones. Its dark shards glittered wickedly.

It's really too bad, Lionel thought, and, compressing his lips angrily, he set off up the garden, determined to have it out with Danny. This time, Nina or no, he would make it clear that the arrangement would have to come to an end. Danny must go by next Saturday at the latest.

He stooped to pick up the broken glass, placing it in the carton, before mounting the steps and knocking at the caravan door. Getting no answer, he pushed it open and entered, fully expecting to find Danny still in bed.

The interior was in semi-darkness and smelt quite dreadful, an odour of stale bedding mingled with sour milk and rotting food. It was also stifling hot, a condition he couldn't account for until he saw the bright orange coil of the electric boiling ring glowing fiercely at the far end. Nostrils pinched together, he swept aside the curtains to reveal the full extent of Danny's depredations.

For a moment he couldn't absorb it all, and he was aware only of a general confusion and squalor, bedclothes flung about, dirty plates and cups everywhere, the tiny kitchen littered with God knows what filth.

His sense of shock and outrage was similar, he imagined, to that which victims of a burglary must experience, not just against their possessions but against their own persons. It was a kind of rape.

As the shock passed, it was replaced by anger. How dare he? How bloody well dare he?

Lips trembling, Lionel clambered across the bed to switch off the electric ring, aware for the first time of the details of Danny's pillage: the ground-in dirt and grit on the sheets, the long, brown scars on the edges of the furniture where cigarettes had been left burning, the ash and stains fouling the carpet. Where the boiling ring had been standing, the plastic-coated counter top had buckled with the heat and the sink was filthy with grease and scraps of food, while the smell emanated, he discovered, from a small regiment of empty tins and unwashed milk bottles clustered together on the draining-board.

It could all be put back in order, of course, the carpet shampooed, the rubbish thrown away, the burn-scars sanded out and varnished over, but that wasn't the point. It would be a long time before he could feel at ease in the place again. Mere scrubbing and repainting wouldn't erase Danny's presence. Nor did he have any intention of beginning on it today. There was something else he had to do first; another and more important exorcism.

Returning to the house, he spread out his portfolio on the floor of his bedroom where his art materials were temporarily housed and, from the back of it, removed a small collection of drawings from their separate paper folder. They were all of Nina, quick sketches made when she was unaware of what he was doing, although some he had worked up later into proper portraits, tinted in with water-colours; Nina laughing, head flung back; Nina pensive, resting her chin on one hand. Shuffling quickly through them, he could remember each occasion when he had made them. In this one, Nina had been asleep in a deck-chair in the garden; high summer with the leaves forming a dense, green background. In the next, she had been bending down to talk to Max one evening, although Max wasn't present in the drawing; just her, with her hair slipping loose and catching the light in fiery points of colour.

None of them was very good. Lionel had seen some of Max's sketches of her and had realised that, compared to those, his own were amateurish. But they were all he had; these and the notes which, over the years, she had pushed through his letter-box, finding him out when she called. Scrawled on any scrap of paper she happened to have on her, they could hardly be called love-letters. He glanced at them again. Requests to come round to help Max out of the bath; the boiler was leaking, did he know anything about plumbing? she'd borrowed the shears to cut the hedge but she'd bring them back tomorrow. All signed, 'Love, Nina.'

Putting them with the sketches, he tore the lot across the middle and, clutching the pieces in one hand, returned to the garden where, just as he was about to consign them to the incinerator, he heard the crackle of cycle wheels on the drive and had only time to fling them inside, bang the lid on top and scuttle back to the house before Nina came hurrying round the corner and, without so much as a glance at his window, went running up the lawn towards the caravan.

After he left Althorpe House, Finch turned right at the gate in the direction of the village and drove a little distance along the road before reversing the car into a narrow lane which, according to the finger-post at its entrance, led to Upfield Farm. A few yards in, he braked and turned off the engine.

The lane opening was obscured by trees but the boundary hedge was low enough to give him an unrestricted view of any traffic passing along the road. After a short wait, he saw what he had been expecting: the head and shoulders of Nina Gifford sailing past with the effortless ease and speed of someone on an unseen bicycle. Allowing her a few minutes' start, he bumped the car slowly down the lane and followed her.

Even if he had not guessed her destination, her bicycle was easily spotted, flung negligently up against the interwoven fence that ran along the side of Lionel Burnett's driveway where, in her haste to get to Danny, she had abandoned it. Burnett's car was standing in the drive, suggesting he was at home, and, as Finch edged sideways past it, he could only hope to God that Burnett would have the sense to make himself scarce.

Lionel, who was keeping well back out of sight behind the kitchen window, had no intention of interfering. First Nina's arrival, followed so quickly by the Chief Inspector's, indicated that something was afoot in which he had no doubt Danny was also implicated and Lionel had no wish to be drawn into it.

Let them sort it out among themselves, he told himself although he grieved for Nina's sake.

All the same, his concern for her did not prevent him from putting on his jacket and, as soon as the coast was clear, letting himself out quietly by the front door; too early by nearly three-quarters of an hour for matins, but he preferred to sit in the porch outside the church to remaining in the cottage and risking a confrontation with either Nina or Finch.

Entering the caravan and finding Danny was not there, Nina was more concerned with the absence of his possessions about the place than its state of confusion to which, in the first frantic moments after her arrival, she added by flinging aside the already tumbled bedclothes and opening cupboards and drawers in the built-in units in an attempt to find something belonging to him.

Nothing. Not even a pair of shoes or his razor.

It was at this point that Finch arrived, mounting the steps to stand in the open doorway, blocking the light, and she turned quickly towards him, her face distraught, momentarily forgetting who he was in her need to confide in someone.

'Danny's gone!' she announced.

'Has he now?' Finch said and stepped inside.

Suddenly aware of the significance of his arrival, Nina plumped down onto the bed and burst into tears.

Finch kept his distance, waiting for the storm of emotion to wear itself out, and looking about him at the squalor. Danny had certainly left his mark on the place. From time to time, he allowed his gaze to rest on her with a professional objectivity, like a doctor observing a patient's symptoms. She was crouching on the low bed, her hands over her face so that only the top of her head was visible, her knees spread out in order to take the weight of her elbows, in the awkward, clumsy posture of a woman who, given over entirely to grief, no longer cares what she looks like.

Finch's cool gaze, however, disguised more emotion than he cared to show. Never at ease with other people's tears, especially a woman's, he felt totally inadequate, a reluctant voyeur of emotions he knew he was partly responsible for but which, as a professional policeman, he had to learn to observe impassively.

Presently her grief subsided into little, gasping sobs and she lifted her face.

'I haven't got a hanky,' she confessed, wiping the back of her hand under her eyes and sniffing deeply.

Finch passed her his as he took a seat beside her on the bed, still taking care to leave plenty of room between them. She rubbed it harshly over her face as if scrubbing away the last dregs of emotion as well as the tears and then sat quietly, waiting for him to begin, the crumpled handkerchief in her lap.

'The sketches,' Finch said simply.

'I gave them to Danny,' she admitted. 'He was hard up and I thought he could sell them and raise a bit of cash for himself. I hadn't any money to give him.'

'Did Max know?'

'No, I took them without asking. I didn't think he'd miss them. He's got hundreds and he hadn't looked at them for months.'

'When was this?'

'Just after Christmas. Danny turned up one day and I gave him four. A few weeks later he wrote asking if I'd got any others and I posted a couple more to him.'

'I see. Go on.'

She was silent for a few seconds before replying ingenuously, 'I can't think of anything else.'

'Can't you, Mrs Gifford?'

'Only that Danny had nothing to do with Eustace Quinn's death, if that's what you're thinking. He can't have done!'

She seemed close to tears again and Finch replied with deliberate brusqueness, the verbal equivalent of the slap round the face recommended in cases of hysteria, 'He knew Eustace Quinn.'

It was her worst fear and, now that it was out in the open, she was able to confront it with more courage than she had thought possible.

'I don't care. It doesn't make any difference. I know Danny didn't do it.'

There was a stubborn, unyielding quality about her which,

although Finch had grudgingly to admire, he had somehow to break down.

'You realise Eustace Quinn wanted to meet Max because of the sketches?'

'Yes, I know that now.'

'Which he'd bought from Danny?'

She admitted that, too. His questions bore down on her like stones, each one adding its own weight so that she felt suffocated by their burden.

'And did you also know that Danny had a police record?'

Finch threw that in for good measure although, in fact, the sum total of this evidence was a charge of careless driving for which he had been fined and the suspicion that he had been involved in a used-car fraud in which nothing had been proved, but Finch had no intention of telling her this.

'I'd guessed,' she replied humbly and seemed oddly grateful that this, too, could now be admitted.

'And you still think he had nothing to do with Quinn's death?'

'Yes!' she cried passionately. 'Because I know him!'

'Ah.' Finch sounded satisfied as if he had at last reached the point he wanted. 'How well do you know him, Mrs Gifford? A little better than a family friend, I think. Am I right?'

'He's my brother.'

The information should not have surprised him, although it did. It was one of the relationships which had occurred to him when he had discussed the matter with Boyce, although he had dismissed it as unlikely.

Now that she had confessed it, she seemed eager to explain, to excuse, perhaps even to talk her way out of it for Danny's sake.

'He's much younger than me and I suppose he's always been difficult, even as a child, but never really wicked, you must believe that. You see, my mother died when he was born and he was brought up by an aunt, my father's sister. She'd never married and I don't think she understood young children. Besides, she had to give up her job – she was a maths teacher in a girls' school – to look after us and she resented it.'

'Couldn't your father afford a housekeeper?' Finch asked.

'God, no! He's a country parson; or rather he was; he's retired now. And anyway, Aunt Connie looked on it as her duty; at least, that's what she was always telling us. "I've tried to do my duty by you children."'

And probably enjoyed the martyrdom, Finch commented silently. He had known women like her who never allowed the obligation owing to them to them to be forgotten and who spent their lives eaten up by bitterness and resentment.

'Part of the trouble was she disapproved of my father's marriage,' Nina continued. 'You see, my mother was years younger than him; a local girl he'd met when he was vicar of another parish, and Aunt Connie thought he'd been a fool to marry her.'

Like mother, like daughter? Finch wondered. It was strange that, in speaking of her mother's marriage to a man older than herself, Nina Gifford did not appear to make any comparison with her own.

Lifting her shoulders as if expressing the inevitability of it all, she added, 'So Danny grew up without any real love except what I could give him, and perhaps,' and here she looked down into her lap at the wet handkerchief which she was turning over and over in her hands, 'it wasn't the sort of love he really needed.'

'How old were you?'

'When my mother died? Nine. As long as I can remember, I always wanted to be like her – a mother to Danny, I mean, but I don't think I was very good at it.'

'It wasn't an easy role for a child to play,' Finch pointed out in her defence.

She shrugged again with that hopeless gesture but didn't answer him.

'What about your father?'

'Oh, Dad! I suppose he did his best, but he was over forty when Danny was born and he didn't want to be bothered. We were left to our own devices a lot of the time.' Smiling at the memory of it, she looked Finch in the face as if challenging him with their old, childhood misdemeanours. 'It was Danny and me against Dad and Aunt Connie. I don't think they knew half of what we got up to when we were on our own.'

Under the circumstances it was understandable, even forgivable behaviour, but a dangerous path, all the same, for Danny, and perhaps even for Nina Gifford herself, to have started out on all those years before. No wonder Danny Webb had turned out to be the man he was: immature, resentful of authority and yet too weak to stand on his own feet for long, still relying, like a child, on his elder sister to help him out of his difficulties. Whether or not his criminal tendencies had led him as far as murder remained to be proved and, with this in mind, Finch decided not to tell her that Danny's alibi did not cover the time of Eustace Quinn's death. He hardly needed to rub her nose in the fact that the evidence against Webb was mounting up, quite satisfactorily from his point of view. Instead, he remarked as he rose to go,

'I suppose you have no idea where he is?'

'I wouldn't be here now if I did!' she flashed back at him.

Which was exactly Finch's own assumption.

'By the way,' he added at the door, 'if Danny should turn up, tell him to be sensible and come along to talk to me. Don't try to hide him. If necessary, I could always get a search warrant, you know.'

The warning, casually stated, was nevertheless not lost on her, for Finch saw her look of alarm as he turned and walked down the steps.

She'd be a fool if she did give him shelter; not that Finch wouldn't put it past her. Her kind of loyalty would stop at nothing and he was prepared, if need be, to carry out his threat and turn Althorpe House over from attic to cellar. He'd certainly arrange for a Panda car to patrol up and down the road in front of the house as a warning to her and her brother, should he still be hanging about the neighbourhood, that he meant business.

At the foot of the steps he paused to button up his coat, for the morning, despite the sunshine, had a late spring chill in it and, as he stood there, a flicker of white on the far side of the garden caught his attention; a piece of paper trapped under the rim of the lid covering an incinerator which stood, decently hidden from the house behind a trellis, on a little, flagstoned patch. His curiosity aroused by its frantic waving, which seemed to be signalling to him, Finch walked across and released it. The right half of Nina Gifford's face looked back at him from the torn sheet. With a rapid, backward glance at the caravan to make sure he wasn't being observed, he took off the lid and plunged in his hand, coming up with a fistful of scraps which he transferred surreptitiously to his pocket before continuing on his way to his car.

Seated inside it, he examined them. They were all drawings of Nina, torn across the middle, some halves of which fitted together to make up the whole portrait. Lionel Burnett's work, Finch decided. Even he could tell they were amateurish. Mixed up with them were pieces of letters, or rather rough scribbled notes, sent, he assumed, by Nina to Lionel, judging by the names on the bits he had salvaged.

Interesting, Finch thought as he smoothed out the creases before putting the fragments into his wallet for safe keeping. They suggested that Lionel Burnett's feeling for Nina Gifford extended far beyond normal attraction. There was something obsessional about them, especially the preserved notes. Would any ordinary lover bother to keep a woman's scrawled messages, particularly on such mundane subjects? The words 'boiler' and 'plumbing' features on one; another seemed to be concerned with a pair of shears.

And why, having preserved them, had Lionel Burnett decided to destroy them? Unless, of course, he had finished with Nina Gifford and, in that case, the reason wasn't difficult to find. Burnett himself had let part of that particular cat out of the bag when he had spoken of Eustace Quinn's familiarity, presumably with Nina Gifford, and it again crossed the Chief Inspector's mind that Burnett had witnessed something of Quinn's deliberate flirtation with Nina when he had called at

Althorpe House on Thursday evening. It made sense and it added up also to a possible motive for murder, far-fetched though it might seem. But a man who made drawings of the woman he loved and hoarded up any scrap of her writing could hardly be judged as normal.

He'd discuss it with Boyce later, Finch decided, starting up the car and driving away, although he could imagine the sergeant's reaction. As far as love was concerned, Boyce's attitude was of the earth earthy: regular meals and clean shirts in exchange for the housekeeping money, with an occasional bunch of flowers awkwardly proffered and sex twice a week with the light off. There was nothing as highfalutin as the word romance in his entire vocabulary.

Nina heard the sound of his car retreating and it brought a little relief. At least he'd gone. She was still seated on the bed, nursing his handkerchief in her lap, thinking about Danny and what on earth she could do for him now. The answer was nothing. Danny had passed out of the range of both her love and her assistance. All that remained was the squalor he had created.

And God, what a mess he had left behind him! Lionel would be furious if he saw it and would blame her for having introduced Danny in the first place. She'd have to do something about clearing it up, which was better, anyway, than simply sitting there brooding.

She began by stripping the bed of its sheets and rolling them up into a bundle, finding mixed up with them one of Danny's dirty socks which she stuffed into her skirt pocket along with Finch's handkerchief before shaking out the blankets and folding back the bed into the sofa-shape it assumed for day-time use.

The floor underneath was filthy with spent cigarette ends and old fluff and, suddenly defeated by it all, she couldn't bring herself to make any further attempt at coping with it. Besides, to do the job properly she'd need hot water and a scrubbing-brush as well as detergents, scouring powder and plastic sacks for collecting up the rubbish.

Searching among the confusion, she found a biro – Danny's, in fact – and a reasonably clean brown paper-bag which she tore open before writing a letter to Lionel on its inner surface, forming the words neatly and legibly instead of dashing off her normal scrawl in the first, small gesture of reconciliation.

'Dear Lionel, I'm so sorry about the mess Danny has made of the caravan but I'll come back this afternoon and clean it all up. Please forgive both of us. Danny has run away because the police are looking for him but don't say anything to Max as it would upset him. I'm very worried about him. Sorry again about everything but I promise to put it right. Love, Nina. P.S. Could I borrow a bucket? I don't think I explained, by the way, that Danny is my brother.'

Taking the note with her, she pushed it through Lionel's letter-box before cramming the sheets into the basket on the front of her bicycle and setting off for home.

Max didn't seem to have missed her, thank God. At least, he made no comment when she took up his mid-morning cup of coffee. As for the rest of the morning, she passed it as best she could, putting the sheets in to soak while she cooked dinner, trying to keep at bay her concern for Danny, although there were occasions when it overwhelmed her. The only comfort she could find was in the thought that he had gone – to London, she hoped, where there would be little chance of Finch finding him. What he'd do for money she had no idea. He'd probably write to her eventually. And perhaps, by then, Eustace Quinn's murderer would be found and Danny would be all right. All right. It seemed an absurdly inadequate phrase and, deep down, she realised that Danny would never really be all right.

She longed to talk about it with someone. Max, of course, was out of the question, but perhaps this afternoon when she saw Lionel that, too, would be *all right* and Lionel would listen as he used to do in the past, nodding his head judiciously from time to time and finding something comfortable and comforting to say to her.

But when she returned to the cottage, she found Lionel was out and both the house and the caravan were locked against her. The barring of the caravan was meant to be a deliberate snub, she realised. Lionel wanted nothing to do with her or her peace offering.

In fact, had she known it, Lionel, returning home from matins and finding her note on the door-mat, had decided there and then to absent himself for the whole afternoon and, as a final gesture, had carried her note to the incinerator where he had added it to the other torn-up mementoes before setting light to the lot of them.

The fact that Danny was her brother made no difference to his own attitude towards her. She still expected him to join with her in a conspiracy to keep the truth from Max and even her sentence, 'I'm very worried about him', contained a characteristic ambivalence, for she hadn't made it clear on whose behalf she was concerned, Max or Danny's. Not that this mattered either. As for Danny's involvement with the police, Lionel could only comment silently to himself that it didn't surprise him in the least.

Having satisfied himself that the flames had done their work, he returned to the house and, after washing his hands thoroughly, got back into his car and drove into Bexford where he treated himself to Sunday lunch and a half bottle of claret at the George Hotel.

Lionel's absence which, Nina realised, was as deliberate as his locking of the caravan, grieved her almost as much as Danny's disappearance. It was another form of running away, this time from her, a double loss which she felt with keen bitterness and, cycling home, it was as much as she could do to hold back the tears.

Everything seemed to be falling to pieces around her; all the old, safe friendships and relationships which she had imagined would remain immutable for ever were breaking up. Even the house, as she re-entered it, seemed subject to the same decay and she was aware, as she hadn't been since Eustace Quinn's arrival, of the shabbiness of her surroundings.

She heard Max shouting her name as she entered the kitchen, his voice echoing down into the hall with the peremptory abruptness of someone who has been calling for attention for some time and she shouted back, 'All right! I'm coming!' with weary exasperation as she toiled up the stairs to his room.

'Where have you been?' he demanded as soon as she entered.

'To Lionel's.'

'You might have told me where you were going.'

'How the hell could I?' she cried, suddenly furiously angry. 'You were bloody well asleep! I left you a note.'

It was still propped up, unread, on his bedside table.

She thought he was going to return the anger. His eyes went very bright as they always did just before he lost his temper but instead he held out his arms to her and said in a voice more tender than she had heard him use for years, 'What's the matter, Nine?'

She fell onto the bed on top of him, making him grunt as she knocked the breath out of his body and, as he put his arms round her and cradled her close, she could hear him making little crooning noises; like some bloody pigeon, she thought ridiculously and didn't know whether to laugh or cry. In the end, she did both while Max rocked her, stroking back her hair with one of his huge hands – a navvy's, not an artist's, as she'd often told him – and finally, when the storm was over, he wiped her face for her on the edge of the sheet.

'Tell me,' he coaxed her when she sat upright again, but she could only shake her head and answer, 'Nothing.'

'It's not nothing, Nine.'

'I'm tired, that's all.'

'Of me?'

'No, of course not.'

'Of looking after me, then?'

'Sometimes,' she admitted. At least she owed him that piece of honesty. 'And the house and the boiler. Don't worry. I'll get over it.'

'But it's not been all bad, has it, Nina? Not all the time?'

He was looking, she realised, for assurance of her love, something he had never done before and she said quickly, 'Oh, Max, how could you even ask?'

'There have been good times?'

'Marvellous times.'

One in particular came into her mind, so bright and intense that it seemed to be stamped in some glittering substance on her memory: a summer Sunday afternoon years ago when five of them had crammed into someone's baby Austin and had driven out to the Sussex Downs for a picnic lunch. Afterwards, surfeited with sun and wine, she had fallen asleep on the grass to be awakened by the sound of laughter and had opened her eyes to find Max kneeling in front of her, holding a crown of flowers in his hands. It must have taken him hours to thread the delicate stems together. His thumb-nail was stained green with the juices. She had knelt, too, she remembered, at his request, unfastening the ribbon which held her hair back so that it came tumbling loose, and then, the others silent now, Max had placed the crown on her head. It had been a supreme moment for her, the apex of their relationship, as if, in crowning her, Max had also crowned their love for each other.

'Do you remember . . . ?' she began and then fell silent. Max had withdrawn again into himself. While she had been kneeling on the grass, wearing her coronet of flowers, where had he been? Not with her, she realised, but somewhere of his own, apart.

He was still holding one of her hands and, as she faltered, he lifted it between both of his and placed it against his chest, but whether to bless or heal some hidden hurt or in unspoken tribute she couldn't decide. His eyes were closed and his face wore that look of exhausted sadness which had become his habitual expression.

She wanted to say something comforting to him about the loss of the exhibition but, feeling it would be an intrusion, she bent, instead, and kissed his forehead and, as she turned at the door to look back at him, she saw he was lying back against the pillows, his eyes shut, and making no sign that he was aware either of her presence or of her imminent departure from the room.

The rest of the day dwindled and died. At dusk, she remembered the sheets were still on the line and, as she unpegged them and folded them down into her arms, a rustle in the bushes behind her startled her and she spun round.

And suddenly there was Danny running across the lawn towards her, dropping his suitcase as he ran and, the next moment, she was hugging him close to her, the sheets crumpled up between them.

'But where have you been all day?' she asked a little later when they were together in the kitchen. She had closed the door into the hall so that Max couldn't hear them talking and had bundled the creased sheets away on the wheelchair.

'I holed up in some barn across the fields. I was coming here to you when that bloody Inspector turned up. Christ, Nine, I'm famished! Have you got something to eat?'

'There's some meat left over from the joint and some cold potatoes I could fry up.'

'Anything'll do. Got any fags as well? I haven't had a cigarette since this morning.'

She broke off her preparations for the meal to find the spare packet of Max's which she kept in the dresser drawer in case he ran out of them when the shop was closed.

'Is this all you've got?' Danny demanded. 'Haven't you any decent ones?'

'Sorry, that's all there is, Danny,' she replied, stricken by the thought of his disappointment.

'Oh, hell, I suppose they'll have to do then. I was going to the Feathers to buy some only there was a bloody police car patrolling up and down the road.'

Nina made no comment, pretending to be busy with the meal, but she felt a surge of anger and fear at the news. Damn Finch! He certainly hadn't wasted any time in putting on the pressure. One thing was clear: she dared not risk hiding Danny indefinitely. Finch would almost certainly make good his threat of searching the house. Danny would have to leave, but when or where to she had no idea.

Decide later, she told herself. Get him fed first; that's the most important thing. I'll worry about the rest afterwards.

He ate ravenously, the cigarette he had lit earlier and hadn't had time to finish smouldering in an ashtray at the side of his plate.

She watched him in silence and only when he had finished and pushed the empty plate away from him did she venture to broach the subject.

'About Finch,' she began tentatively.

'What about him?'

'Danny, he's looking for you!'

There was no other way she could think of saying it. However much she wrapped it up in words, the truth would have to come out eventually. Besides, for Danny's sake, it was better that he knew exactly where he stood.

She saw his face go very still and quiet as it always used to when, as a child, he had been faced with irrefutable evidence of some misdemeanour.

'He knows I've cleared out?' he asked.

'Yes.'

'Oh, bloody hell!'

'It was my fault, Danny!' she cried. 'You see, he came here with those sketches. You know the ones I mean? I thought I'd better warn you he'd got them.'

'Don't tell me,' Danny interrupted with a little, sneering laugh. 'He followed you. For Christ's sake, Nine, it's the oldest bloody trick in the book and you fell for it!'

'I'm sorry,' she said humbly. 'I just didn't think.'

'Well, the harm's done now. What else does he know?'

'He knows you sold Eustace Quinn the sketches and it was because of them that Quinn wanted to meet Max. Oh, Danny, I think Finch suspects you might have killed him! You didn't, did you? I know you weren't in the caravan that morning . . .'

'How do you know that?'

'I went to the cottage to phone the police and . . .'

'Does anyone else know?'

'Yes, Lionel.'

'That nurk!'

'It was Lionel who told me you weren't there when I called. Danny, where were you?'

'I was down at the Feathers.'

'All morning?'

'Yes, of course. I was there when the landlord opened the bloody place up.'

It sounded genuine, but she had never been able to tell when he was lying or telling the truth.

Before she had time to question him further, he added, 'Does Finch know – about me not being in the caravan, I mean?'

'Yes. He wanted to know about you on Friday afternoon when you came to the house. I said you were down at the pub . . .'

'Shit!' Danny got up violently from the table and began to prowl up and down the kitchen, lighting a new cigarette from the butt of the old one which he pitched at the boiler. 'Shut up, Nina,' he told her as she started to speak. 'I've got to think this out.'

But she couldn't remain silent.

'Danny, I've been so terribly worried! Why did you leave London? Has that got anything to do with Eustace Quinn?'

He looked at her with genuine astonishment.

'I told you, I owed some blokes some money.'

'Is that true?'

'Yes, for God's sake! What do you want – a fucking signed statement? I got into a poker game and lost more than I meant to. They threatened to send the mob round if I didn't pay up so I cleared out.'

'How much?' she asked to check the truth of what he was telling her.

'Three hundred quid.'

'But you told me one!' This minor point seemed ridiculously important.

'One! Three! What the hell difference does it make? I still bloody owe it.'

Chastened, she sat quietly for a few moments, following him with her eyes as he paced up and down, knowing that the question she had already asked once and which he hadn't answered would have to be repeated.

'Did you, Danny?'

'Did I what?'

She lost her temper as she had done earlier with Max but this time there was no question of her bursting into tears. Inside, she felt quite dry and rigid.

'You know damn well what I mean! Did you kill Eustace Quinn? And don't lie to me. I must know the truth. If you did it, it won't make any difference but, in God's name, I have to know!'

He came immediately across the kitchen to her, squatting down in front of her and placing his hands on her knees to keep his balance as he tipped back his head to look her in the face.

'Oh, Nina, what a question! Of course I didn't!'

His eyes were stretched wide, showing a rim of white round the irises, and she searched them for any sign of falsehood. But she still wasn't sure.

'Honest Injun?' she asked, using the childhood formula which he remembered and completed.

'Cross my heart and hope to die.'

And with that she had to be satisfied.

'So what about a last cup of tea then?' he asked, springing to his feet, quite sure he had convinced her and nothing more need be said. 'Only I was up at some God-awful hour this morning and I could do with an early night.'

The mention of tea reminded her of Max and she made a big potful, enough for the three of them, before carrying Max's supper upstairs – a boiled egg and bread and butter for, since he had taken to his bed, he seemed not to want much to eat.

'Is anyone downstairs with you?' he asked suspiciously as she laid the tray across his knees.

'No,' she lied quickly.

'I thought I heard voices earlier.'

'I had the radio on, that's all.'

It seemed to satisfy him for he turned to his supper, cracking the top of the egg with a whack from the back of the spoon.

Ordinarily, she would have stayed while he ate, sitting on the bed while she waited to take the tray away, and they would talk together although, even at the best of times, Max had never had the patience for desultory chat and it was usually she who provided most of the conversation.

This evening, maddeningly, when she wanted to get back to Danny, it was he who wanted to keep her. And how slowly he ate! Each spoonful of egg was carefully scooped from the shell. Between mouthfuls, he asked a question or made some remark with the same slow deliberation. Did she feel better now? Really? Was she sure? Perhaps she ought to see that old quack, Foreman, and get a tonic although, in his opinion, there was nothing to beat a drop of champagne.

'Treat yourself to a bottle, Nine,' he told her, wagging his egg-spoon at her.

And where the hell did he imagine the money was coming from to pay for it? she thought impatiently.

'I've got to fetch something, Max,' she said, finding it impossible to sit there any longer. 'I'll only be five minutes. Finish your supper.'

As she grabbed up blankets and a pillow from one of the spare beds, it suddenly occurred to her what to do about Danny. She could send him to Zoe's! Zoe knew nothing about Eustace Quinn's murder and surely she'd be willing to put Danny up for a few days. It was safer than a hotel, too. It was the last place that Finch would think of looking for him and she'd know herself where he was, at least for the time being. But he'd have to leave early, before there was any chance of Finch turning up to make good his threat to search the house.

Dumping the bedding in the hall, she hurried back upstairs to Max, who had finished his supper and was waiting for her.

Getting him to the bathroom and back seemed to take hours. Then she had to settle him into bed, give him his pills and plump up his pillows before she could finally leave him for the night. Bending down to kiss him, she was overcome with a pang of guilt. Poor Max! Her haste to leave him was almost like a betrayal.

Downstairs, she forgot him in her concern for Danny. Knowing him, everything would have to be cut and dried otherwise he'd argue but, once presented with a complete plan of action, he'd fall in with her wishes. It had been the same when they were children. She had only to say, 'Listen, this is what we'll do,' giving him no option, and he would agree.

First there was the rates money, which she kept hidden in a vase in the sitting-room; sixty-five pounds altogether, though she thought fifty should be enough. Returning the fifteen to the vase, she wondered what the hell she would do when the rates fell due. But that seemed unimportant. Something would turn up. If the worst came to the worst, she'd do as Danny had done and sell some of Max's sketches in London.

If only that damned exhibition had come off, they'd all be sitting pretty. There'd be money coming in, Max would be happy and Danny wouldn't be in this God-awful mess. But it couldn't be helped.

Shrugging, she found paper and pen for the letter to Zoe, looked up the local bus timetable and made up Danny's bed on the sofa, safer than letting him sleep upstairs where Max might hear him. As a final, welcoming gesture, she turned on the electric fire so that the room would be warm for him before returning to the kitchen.

'Christ, Nina,' Danny said as she entered. 'You've been gone for bloody ages.'

'I've had things to do,' she told him. She felt strong and confident as she placed glasses on the table.

'What are those for?' he asked.

'What do you think, you idiot? We're going to have a little celebration,' she replied, fetching the bottle of brandy and pouring drinks for them both. 'While I've been gone, I've been thinking about what you can do and I've got it all beautifully worked out, so listen. You stay here tonight and then, in the morning, I'll wake you up early and we'll walk across the fields to the Millstead road. There's a bus at five past seven that'll take you into Millstead in time to catch the 8.55 Green-line coach to London.' He began to demur at the early start but she overrode his protestations. 'Don't be a fool, Danny. You've got to be out of the house in case the police come. And don't you see? They'll be watching this road and the buses into Bexford, expecting you to catch a train to London from there.'

'Yes, I can see that,' he admitted grudgingly. 'But what the hell do I do when I get to London?'

'It's all organised. You go to Zoe's, Max's ex-wife. In fact, I've already asked her to look out for a flat for you so she knows a bit about you. But never mind that now. The point is, she's got a sofa in her living-room you could sleep on for a few days until you can get yourself a job and somewhere else to live. Look, I've written her a letter and I'm putting twenty-five pounds in it. That's for her. The other twenty-five's for you. I know it isn't much but it'll keep you going for the time being.' Before handing it over to him, she licked the flap of the envelope and stuck it down, not so much because she didn't trust him as to reassure Zoe that the money was intact. 'Her address is on the front. And for God's sake don't lose it!'

'I won't,' he promised, putting both the envelope and the money into his wallet. 'Thanks, Nine.'

'And don't tell her more than you have to,' Nina added. 'She's a nosey old bitch so watch out. I told her, by the way, that you're a friend so don't let on, will you?'

'Are you sure she'll have me?' he asked.

'Oh, yes.' Nina sounded quite confident. 'For twenty-five quid, Zoe'd let Dracula sleep on her sofa.'

The absurdity of the idea struck them at the same time and they burst out laughing together, Danny gripping her wrist in the pleasure of their shared amusement.

'God, Nina, you're a bloody marvel!' he told her. 'You could always fix things.'

'Like the old days?' she asked. 'Remember the time we put that balloon in with the fruit at the Harvest Festival?'

'And the bloody thing came loose during the blessing and floated down from the edge of the pulpit?'

'Dad's face!'

'And Aunt Connie's!'

'Sh! Sh!' she warned him, still laughing and pointing up towards the ceiling to remind him of Max's presence in the house and, as they muffled their laughter, she felt again that sharp pang of guilt which had touched her earlier.

As in the past when they were children, it was still she and Danny in league against authority, only this time they were joining hands together against Max, forming their own circle to exclude him and from the centre of which he was banished.

13

The alarm clock woke Nina at five the following morning and she got out of bed and dressed, making as little noise as possible so as not to disturb Max. Closing his door as she passed it on the landing, she could hear, inside the room, his deep, rumbling breathing.

Downstairs, she made Danny's breakfast and carried the tray into the sitting-room. He slept more quietly than Max, lying in the same position she remembered he had always assumed as a child, curled up like a foetus under the bedclothes, one hand stuffed beneath the pillow. He woke in the same manner as he used to, opening his eyes as she gently shook his shoulder and staring straight ahead for a few seconds without moving, as if accustoming himself to the sensation of wakefulness.

'Breakfast, Danny,' she said in a low voice.

They set off at six, leaving by the shrubbery gate and striking off across the fields, Nina in front, Danny behind.

The sun had risen but had not yet dispersed the early morning mist which was looped between the trees in nets of gauzy light reducing perspective and distance so that they seemed to be walking through a tent of golden muslin spun from airy filaments. A rich bloom of dew was lying on the grass and the leaves were matt with moisture.

How silent it is! Nina thought. Their footsteps were absorbed into the wet grass so that they themselves became part of the stillness. She was awed by the silence and the luminous beauty of the morning.

At the far side of the field, she turned and waited for Danny to catch up with her. He walked awkwardly in his city shoes, lugging his suitcase, his features bunched up tightly with misery and discomfort.

Why wasn't he moved by the same delight? Nina wondered, although her heart went out to him.

Behind him, until lost in the hazy dazzle, stretched a line of dark prints where their feet had smudged the dew.

'How much further is it?' he asked as he drew alongside her.

'About another mile and a half,' she replied. Not even his bad mood could entirely destroy her own sense of peace and serenity.

'Christ! That far? My bloody feet are soaking wet already.'

Without replying, she turned and began to walk on again. The moisture had coated her eyelashes so that, looking through them, the mist seemed doubly diaphanous and everything around her, the outlines of the trees, the distant hedges, appeared to be dissolving and melting away. It was like Max's last painting, she realised, the one in which Lilith had been on the point of vanishing, and, for a rare instance, Nina felt that she could see with Max's eyes, a sensation she had never experienced before.

But not for long for, as they walked on, the sunlight strengthened and the mist gradually disappeared, licked away, it seemed, by the warmth. Little by little, outlines grew stronger, distances reasserted themselves, shapes moved forward so that by the time they reached the Millstead road all that was left was small pockets of white vapour clinging in hollows and a vague, watery aura along the horizon. The sun was now so bright that it hurt their eyes.

There was only ten minutes to wait before the bus was due and, as they climbed over the gate into the road, Nina had ready in her mind half a dozen last-minute things that she wanted to say to Danny but he didn't give her time for any of them, not even to repeat the warning about Zoe. As they neared the bus-stop, he said, 'Don't come any further, Nina,' in a voice that couldn't be ignored. He gave her his cheek to kiss, the rest of his face being turned deliberately away from her. His skin was cold to her lips.

'Write to me,' she begged and that was all she had the chance to say. He had walked off before she could add anything else and there was nothing she could do except retrace her steps to the gate where she paused to look back at him, even though she knew he would not turn to wave.

He was standing with his back to her, looking up the road in the direction from which the bus would come, one hand in his pocket, the other still holding onto his shabby suitcase, hunching his shoulders forward in his familiar, defensive stance which gave his figure, outlined against the sun, the silhouette of hopeless dejection, like a man in a dole queue or a refugee waiting for a cattle-truck that was to take him into exile.

Finch also watched the mist disperse. He had stayed late in the office the previous evening, organising the search for Danny Webb before catching up with the paper-work involved in the case and, at three o'clock in the morning, had decided it was not worth going home. Anyway, there was no one to go home to. His widowed sister, Dorothy, who kept house for him had gone to visit an old schoolfriend, also widowed, in Cambridge, and he wondered again as he had many times in the past if, without him to take care of, she might not have made a better life for herself with Barbara. She liked Cambridge; the two women appeared to enjoy each other's company; Dorothy was certainly a different person when she returned home from these visits, more animated but also anxious that, in her absence, he hadn't been looking after himself properly. Nina's remarks about her aunt had reawakened his own feelings of guilt about his sister. Did she, too, only stay out of a sense of duty? There was no way of finding out, for he could hardly ask her. Their relationship was based almost entirely on what was not said between them.

At times like this he half-regretted never having married,

even though he realised it was too late to make the commitment. The passion which might once have swept him into it had been channelled into his work and now he was not sure that he was capable of redirecting it. Like storm water, it had been caught and tamed before he had allowed it to overwhelm him and the runnels he had dug for it were too deep and too entrenched by custom for it ever to break their banks. And yet, he was not quite without susceptibilities. He remembered Blanche Lester's arm trembling in his as they walked together in the park, the dip and sway of Nina Gifford's skirt as she bent to fold the washing, and the firm, brown flesh of her hands.

There was room in his heart for someone like Nina, he acknowledged. But not for her. There were too many qualities in her, and in him, that he saw with an objective eye which, like the Cyclops', never seemed to sleep, would lead inevitably to the nagging itch of mutual exasperation; although it would have to be someone like her who could, as she did, shower a radiance about her and disturb the air with the living vitality of her presence.

Meanwhile, in the absence of all feminine influence in his life, including his sister's, he settled down with a blanket on the shabby armchair he kept in the office for such occasions. He slept only fitfully, waking at intervals to hear the distant echoes of a building only partly occupied: voices in a corridor, a door shutting, the ringing of a telephone which went on and on until it was silenced in mid-peal like a scream suddenly cut short.

At six o'clock he gave up the pretence of sleeping any longer and made himself coffee, which he drank standing at the window. The sun was emerging from behind the mist, giving the rooftops opposite a dull, metallic sheen like gunmetal, and behind the haze there was the feeling of the town waking up. Unseen traffic moved along the streets. People were up and about. He felt that if he listened hard enough he might hear their footsteps on the pavements.

Boyce arrived at eight o'clock. By that time Finch had washed and shaved in the men's cloakroom and was sitting at his desk, ready for the day's work, the first half hour of which was taken up with giving the sergeant a brief summary of what had happened over the weekend, after Boyce had reported that no one at Medlave could remember seeing Blanche Lester's Mini passing through the village on the morning of the murder.

'So you think Danny Webb might have murdered Quinn?' Boyce asked when Finch had finished his account.

'I don't know,' Finch confessed. 'He certainly had the opportunity. As we know, he didn't arrive at the Feathers until half past eleven, which would have given him plenty of time to slip into the grounds of Althorpe House through the shrubbery, clobber Quinn and clear off again before Nina Gifford came home. But I can't see he had much of a motive. Admittedly he knew Quinn; in fact, he sold him Max Gifford's sketches but, by my reckoning, that's not sufficient reason for wanting him dead. We'll have to pick him up, of course, if we can, although my bet is he's cleared off back to London so it's not going to be easy. By the way, I've arranged for a couple of plain-clothes men to watch the London trains out of Bexford and I'm sending Marsh and Simpson over to the village to find out from Lionel Burnett if he knows exactly when Webb did his bunk and to make a few inquiries locally in case anyone saw him.'

'What about his sister?' Boyce asked. 'Any chance she might be hiding him?'

'I doubt it. I warned her yesterday that I'd get a search warrant, and unless she's a damned sight more stupid than I think she is she won't risk it. We may still have to search the place but I'm inclined to play that down for a day or two. Let her start feeling secure and then we'll move in. If we haven't found Webb by then, he may have doubled back to Althorpe House, thinking the coast's clear.'

'Clever,' Boyce commented.

'Not particularly. Just common sense. Besides, if we put it off for the time being, we may even have turned up enough new evidence to pin the murder on him as well.'

'And the others?'

'You mean Burnett and the two women? Well, the same applies to them – opportunity but not much in the way of motive. Lionel Burnett is clearly obsessed by Nina Gifford. We've only to take a look at those torn-up drawings and notes he dumped in the incinerator to see that. We also know from Blanche Lester's evidence that Quinn was deliberately flirting with Nina Gifford on Thursday, which I suspect Burnett witnessed or, at least, part of it. I know jealousy can be a strong motive for murder but, as you pointed out, the timing's a bit short for a homicidal passion to work itself up. Still, it's possible so we can't rule him out. As for Blanche Lester, she admits she quarrelled with Quinn on Friday morning about their relationship not long before he was found dead, but unless she's a lot more round the bend than she actually appears, I can't see that giving her enough reason for wanting him dead; not to plan it in cold blood, anyhow, which is what she must have done if we go by the evidence we have against her. We'll have to keep her in mind, of course. And the same goes for Nina Gifford. According to both Blanche and Zoe Hamilton, Quinn was curious about her past and we may find a motive there if we dig about a bit. Which is what I want you to do today, Tom. Go to the Registry of Births and Marriages at St Catherine's House in Kingsway and turn up the records on her. For a start, you can check the date she married Gifford and how old she was at the time.'

'You're thinking it was possibly an illegal marriage?'

'I don't know, but until I've collected a few facts together I've got nothing to go on. So, as far as she's concerned, we'll start from square one and work from there. From what she told Blanche Lester, she was seventeen when she met Max Gifford and ran away with him, so start by checking the entries for the early fifties. As she must be in her forties, it's the earliest date she and Gifford could have married, according to my calculations.'

'Is that all you want me to cover?'

'No, it isn't,' Finch replied, handing Boyce two copies of Miss Martin's list which he had laboriously retyped the evening before, placing half the names on one sheet, half on the other. 'While you're in London, I want you to go down these names individually. They're all people Quinn was in touch with since January when he bought the first of the Gifford drawings. Basically, there's one question you need to ask each of them in turn, and it's this: Did Quinn ever suggest a partnership to mount Gifford's exhibition or any kind of deal connected with it? I've got a hunch it could be important. Quinn mentioned a partner only to Max Gifford; not to Blanche Lester or Miss Martin, his secretary, and I want to find out why.'

'Right,' Boyce said absent-mindedly. As Finch was speaking, he had begun to scan the list and now he looked up, his expression incredulous.

'Just a minute!' he protested. 'Am I supposed to see every man jack of them you've written down here?'

'That's the idea.'

'On my tod? But there's nearly forty of them!'

'Take Kyle with you. He can cover one of the lists.'

'Is that all? What about Marsh?'

'I was planning on sending him along with you but I can't now. He's involved with the inquiries in Althorpe.'

'Oh, hell, yes; I'd forgotten. Then what about Harding or Barney?'

'They're on surveillance at Bexford station. And before you try any more names, Grainger's off sick, Johnson's on leave, Cunningham hasn't had enough experience yet for this type of work and Meredith and that other DC who's just transferred from Thames force, the tall chap with the sideburns . . .'

'Bannister?'

'Yes, well, he's gone with Meredith and the others on that burglary case over at High Watton. Which leaves you and Kyle, I'm afraid, Tom.'

'You realise it's going to take us a couple of days to get through this lot?'

'So I would imagine,' Finch replied equably. 'So you'd better get started. Round Kyle up and, listen, before you go, I want you to phone me every hour, on the hour, do you understand? Kyle can do the same at ten past but I want to know as soon as possible when you turn up Quinn's partner. I'll be here in the office all day, waiting for the various reports to come in. If I get called out, leave a message with the desk sergeant. I'll phone in myself every hour.'

Boyce departed, sighing gustily, and, as the door was about to close behind him, Finch nearly called him back to add a rider instructing him to start his inquiries with Bruce Lawford and then changed his mind. If Bruce Lawford was to have any significance in the inquiry then he must be arrived at through the due process of the investigation.

The first call came at ten o'clock from Boyce, who merely gave the information that, so far, he had been to the Records Office in Kingsway where the staff had undertaken to check through the entries for him. Apart from that, there had only been enough time to call on two people on the list and neither of these knew anything about a partnership with Quinn. Kyle telephoned ten minutes later to report the same negative result. So, too, did their next calls at eleven and ten past. By this time, they had between them visited eight people.

Replacing the receiver after talking to Kyle, Finch took a surreptitious peep at the original list which he had kept by him on the desk. At the rate they were going, it was going to take at least another two hours before Boyce, on whose copy Bruce Lawford's name appeared, had worked his way down to him.

With a gesture of impatience, Finch turned the list face down and fed another sheet of paper into the typewriter, shooting back the sleeves of his jacket before picking out letter by letter the words, '. . . but when I arrived at the caravan, Danny Webb had already gone . . .'

'Fancy another?' Danny asked.

'Thanks, dear, I'd love one,' Zoe replied, as she pushed her empty glass in his direction. She had seen his full wallet and didn't see why she should offer to fork out.

It was just after twelve o'clock and they were seated together in the saloon bar of the Lamb, near Fulham Broadway, a public house which Zoe did not normally frequent but which she had chosen to take Danny to for a snack lunch and a drink shortly after his arrival. As he stood at the bar, waiting to order the second round, she watched his back speculatively.

His arrival a short time earlier had been totally unexpected and her first reaction, until she read Nina's letter with the twenty-five quid in it, had been to say no. She didn't want anyone moving in with her; certainly not someone like him. She knew his type. He'd lounge about the place all day and it'd be a hell of a job ever getting rid of him. Besides, why should she do Nina a good turn? She'd got a bloody nerve to expect any favours in the first place.

But as she stood reading the letter, two sentences had made her change her mind. Nina had written, 'If you could put Danny up for a few days, I'd be very grateful. As I explained to you when I saw you last, he's a friend and he's looking for a flat.'

Nina's gratitude hadn't meant a thing to Zoe but the name had. Danny. It was the same name that the little fat bloke, the man who'd come with Mr Johnson to collect the painting, had mentioned and which Finch had seemed interested in when he was nosing round asking questions on Saturday.

Even then Zoe might have let it pass. She had no particular wish to become involved. The police could do their own dirty work.

It was something that Danny let slip which finally decided her. As she stood there with the letter in her hand, he had remarked, 'My sister seemed to think you wouldn't mind if I kipped down on your sofa.'

'All right then, dear. You can stay,' Zoe had told him, stuffing the letter and the money into her handbag.

Even now, watching him return from the bar with his whisky and her gin and orange, Nina's deception still rankled. Her bloody brother! And she hadn't let on, pretending he was a friend, the lying cow!

'Cheers!' Zoe said, raising her glass.

'Here's mud in your eye,' Danny replied. It was meant as a joke, an awkward attempt to lighten the situation. Zoe knew he was embarrassed to be seen sitting there drinking with her. All the time, he was taking little furtive glances round the place, wondering if anyone was commenting on the pair of them – the old woman with the much younger man, and she laughed with deliberate shrillness and laid a hand on his arm. Heads turned and she saw his face darken.

Draining her glass, she gathered up her handbag.

'Shan't be long dear,' she said, bending down to put her mouth close to his ear in a conspiratorial whisper. 'I've got to go to the you-know-where. I'll be back in a minute.'

The public telephone was in the passage leading to the toilets. With her bag clutched tightly under her arm, Zoe dialled the number and, having given her message, replaced the receiver and went on down the passage, leaving by the emergency door at the far end which led into the yard.

The message was passed on to Finch at a quarter to one, but he waited until Boyce had phoned through before taking any action.

'Listen,' the sergeant began, 'they've turned up something interesting at Records . . .'

'Tell me later,' Finch interrupted. 'I'm coming up to London myself. Fulham police have just phoned me. They've got Danny Webb. I want you to meet me outside Fulham police station at half past two. I ought to be there by then.'

'*Fulham* police? How the hell did they get hold of him?'

'I'll explain when I see you,' Finch said and rang off.

Boyce was waiting for him on the pavement and they entered the building together.

'So?' Boyce asked as if their previous conversation had only just taken place. 'How was it they managed to nab him?'

'Zoe Hamilton, Max Gifford's ex-wife, must have turned him in,' Finch explained. 'It seems Nina Gifford sent Danny to her. Chief Superintendent Blakeny who's in charge said it was an anonymous tip-off, but it can't be anyone else except her. She lives in the area, she knows Nina and the name Danny cropped up when Quinn bought that picture off her. She must have put two and two together. A very shrewd old bird is Zoe.'

'It's saved us a lot of sweat,' Boyce pointed out.

'Knowing her, I doubt if her reasons were that public-spirited. She was simply grabbing the chance to pay off an old score,' Finch replied. The irony of the situation had already occurred to him. For Danny's sake, Nina had turned in desperation for help to the one person she could think of who might shelter him, not realising that Zoe, already apprised of some of the facts of the case through his own interview with her, would turn him over to the police. He added, 'Any luck yet with Quinn's partner?'

'Not so far, but Records have come up with something interesting,' Boyce said, eager to get his oar in. 'There's no entry for Nina Gifford's marriage.'

He looked gratified when Finch stopped in his tracks.

'None? Are you sure?'

'Positive. They checked back to the late forties, further back even than the date you suggested, and there's nothing. Gifford was divorced in '37 all right but there's no record of his remarriage. You realise, of course, that it could give Nina Gifford a motive for murdering Quinn? I mean, supposing he threatened her with something in her past that she didn't want Max Gifford to know about; a lover, say. You said Quinn had been asking questions about her. She might have been afraid that, if Gifford knew, he'd change his will and she'd get nothing, not even the house . . .'

'But even a common-law wife would be legally entitled to inherit. After all, they've been living together for nearly thirty years, longer than a lot of marriages.'

'Did she know that, though?' Boyce asked.

It was a reasonable point that Finch had to concede, for it did indeed give Nina Gifford a very good motive for murder. Faced with the fear that, after a lifetime of caring for Max, she might, at his death, be virtually homeless and penniless, she could very well have decided to silence Quinn. There was, however, still one point that didn't make sense which he voiced aloud to Boyce.

'But why the hell didn't they get married? Max Gifford was free; you said yourself the records show he divorced Zoe, so there was nothing to stop him.'

Boyce shrugged.

'Don't ask me. Perhaps he'd had a bellyful the first time round and didn't fancy a repeat performance. Besides, he's an artist, isn't he? You know what they're like. They shack up with the latest girl-friend for a few months and then move out again when it suits them.'

It was a gross distortion of what, in fact, had happened in Max Gifford's case although Finch didn't bother to point out to the sergeant that, contrary to his description, the Giffords had remained together for over quarter of a century. He had long ago realised that Boyce was in the habit of making certain snap judgements which nothing would change. Mention the word 'artist' and he'd come up, like a cash register, with an automatic response: long hair, sandals and an irregular sex-life.

There wasn't time, anyway, to defend the Giffords. He and Boyce had reached the door of the interview room where Danny Webb was waiting for them.

He was sitting dejectedly on one of the regulation chairs with which the room was furnished, a full ashtray on the table in front of him. A police constable, standing just inside the door, came to attention as the two men entered and Finch dismissed him with a nod.

'Well, Mr Webb, you've led us a bit of a dance,' the Chief Inspector remarked pleasantly, drawing up a chair as Boyce, seating himself beside him, ostentatiously took out his notebook and pen which he placed on the scarred table-top. Years of working together had polished their performance to a perfectly synchronised double act in which their roles were clearly defined, Finch playing the friendly, neighbourhood copper, anxious to see justice done, while Boyce assumed the part of the heavy, a mute but massive reminder of the full weight of the law.

'Who shopped me?' Danny demanded furiously. 'It was that bloody old bitch, wasn't it?'

'It was an anonymous tip-off,' Finch replied, showing no reaction to Danny's anger. It was as much an act as their own, a defensive pose to hide his fear. Finch had smelt it as soon as he entered the room, a faint aroma that was impossible to describe but which to him, as to any creature with a hunter's instinct, was distinct and instantly recognisable: a slightly sour, rancid odour compounded of human sweat and the sharper, more feral secretion of the fear itself. 'But since you're here, by whatever means, I'd like a statement from you.'

'Are you going to charge me?'

'Not yet. I'd like to hear what you've got to say for yourself first. Let's start with these, shall we?' Finch laid the sketches out in front of Webb who looked at them but didn't touch them, anxious not to leave his prints on them, Finch assumed, although that wasn't going to help him much when his own sister's evidence as well as Askew's had already established that they had been in his possession.

'Well?' he continued, as Danny did not answer. 'Come on, Mr Webb. You're not doing your own case any good. Do you want me to start the ball rolling for you? Your sister, Mrs Gifford, gave them to you a few months ago. Am I right?'

'All right, then, she did,' Danny conceded reluctantly and stopped again, watching the sergeant's pen also come to a halt as if its tip was connected to his own tongue and the one set the other in motion. Unsure of exactly how much Finch knew, he was unwilling to say too much. His first instinct had been to deny everything, even his acquaintanceship with Quinn, but it was obvious that Finch had picked up some information from Nina and he felt his fear turn to anger, not so much against the Chief Inspector, although he would have liked to wipe that stupid bloody smile off his face, but against his sister. She'd bleeding well fixed things properly for him, hadn't she? Sending him off to that sodding old cow who'd only waited long enough to pocket the money before turning him in.

'And then you took them along to Mr Askew's, where you later met Mr Quinn,' Finch continued.

Now it was out in the open, Danny saw no point in holding

back. He'd do better to talk, to minimise his own part in the whole bloody business. That way, he'd show he was willing to co-operate, which mightn't be a bad thing.

'That's right, but I only met him once,' he admitted. 'Askew fixed up the meeting. I went round to his shop one evening. Quinn said he was interested in the sketches and he was keen to find out about Max.'

'But you'd never, in fact, met him?'

'Max? No. Nina did a bolt with him when I was about eight; cleared off to London, or so I understood from the odds and sods of gossip I picked up in the village. It was never discussed at home. My father told me not to mention her name again.'

'But she kept in touch with you?'

'Through one of the boys I knew at school. She used to write to his house. Later, when I came up to London, we'd meet from time to time but she never took me back with her.'

'Do you know why?'

Danny shrugged.

'She said it was better that way. Max wasn't the sort who wanted to be mixed up with other people's relations. Besides, she liked keeping things secret. Dad and Aunt Connie didn't know half the things she got up to on the quiet.'

This sly dig at Nina, his own sister, reminded Finch of Zoe Hamilton's smear tactics and he would have preferred to ignore it, but he couldn't.

'What sort of things?'

'Seeing boys in the evenings without them knowing. She used to say she was going to the Youth Club and then slip out and meet them round the back of the church.'

If that was all, then a great number of teenage girls were equally guilty, Finch thought. From the little he knew of her home background, he could imagine that such deceit would have been a necessary subterfuge, especially for someone like Nina Gifford who, even when young, must have had a normal, healthy interest in the opposite sex.

'And you kept in touch with her after she and Max moved to Althorpe?'

'On and off,' Danny replied. 'I'd write and we'd meet in the summer-house at a prearranged time or she'd come up to London occasionally.'

'I see. Now let's get back to Eustace Quinn, shall we?'

'I've told you all I know. Like I said, I only met him the once.'

'But you gave him Max Gifford's address?'

'Yes. Why not?'

'And talked about Max?'

'A bit. There wasn't much I could tell him.'

'What about your sister? Did you discuss her?'

'Quinn seemed interested, so I told him what I knew.'

'What sort of things?'

'About her running away from home with Max when she was still at school and Dad being a country vicar.'

'Where was his parish?'

Finch asked the question casually, although he was curious to find out where Nina had lived as a girl. If Quinn had been interested in her past, then it might be worth while to go back there himself and make a few inquiries in the place where she had grown up.

'Heversham. It's near the Herts-Essex border, a few miles east of Bishops Stortford. Dad's retired now but he and Aunt Connie are still living in the village.'

'Go on. What else did you tell Eustace Quinn?'

'That she'd only known him three days before she ran off with him and that she was under age. There didn't seem any harm in telling him. Besides, I thought it might do her a bit of good.'

Quite how he had reached the conclusion wasn't clear, and Finch suspected that he had talked from the much less altruistic motive that whatever good Quinn had to offer would be coming his way rather than hers.

'Did Quinn mention a possible exhibition of Gifford's work?'

'No, I didn't know anything about that. He didn't tell me,' Danny protested and here, at least, Finch believed he was telling the truth. Danny's voice had the tone of authentic outrage. In order to keep prices low, Quinn had obviously informed none of the people from whom he had bought Gifford's paintings that an exhibition was planned. If he had, Danny, and Zoe also, would have asked for much more money than they had, in fact, been given.

Finch couldn't resist asking, 'What did you get for the sketches?'

His suspicions were confirmed when Danny answered sulkily, 'A fiver each except for the signed ones. I got a tenner for those.'

From what Danny had already said, the next question would be superfluous, but Finch asked it all the same.

'Did Quinn mention a partner to you?'

'No. No one else was in on the deal as far as I knew, except Askew.'

'Right, Mr Webb. Now, I'd like to come to the more recent events of this week. Tell me exactly what happened and what you were doing in Althorpe.'

'I wrote to Nina and told her I was coming down to see her. I'd got into a bit of trouble over a gambling debt so I thought I'd better clear out of London for the time being. I put up at the Dolphin in Bexford for a few days and then went to see Nina.'

'When?'

'Monday morning. We met in the summer-house and she said she'd try to find me another flat in London. Meanwhile she fixed it up for me to stay in Lionel Burnett's caravan.'

'When did you move in?'

'Wednesday. She left a note for me at the Dolphin. Honest to God, I had no idea Quinn was going to turn up the next day. Nine said nothing to me about it. In fact, until Lionel told me someone called Quinn had been murdered, I didn't even know he'd been to see Max.'

'When did Mr Burnett tell you?'

'Friday afternoon. He came back from Nina's just as I turned up from the Feathers and described what had happened. Well, Christ! you can imagine what I felt like when I heard.'

He looked at Finch with shame-faced appeal, his reluctance

to entreat the Chief Inspector's sympathy overcome by his desperation to be believed. Finch could see why Nina went on supporting him. There was the hopelessness of the born loser about him which would arouse her protective instinct. Unlike her, Danny would never survive on his own, though he'd probably not need to. There would always be someone, usually a woman, who would undertake to look after him.

'So you decided to come to the house?' Finch asked, leaving the appeal unanswered.

'I had to risk it. Lionel hadn't told me much, just the bare facts, and I didn't like to question him too far in case he got suspicious. I had to find out more from Nina to know if I was in the clear or not. I walked past the house and couldn't see much sign of anything going on, so I came up the drive to the yard, hoping to attract her attention.'

'Instead of which you attracted mine,' Finch completed the sentence for him in his blandest manner. Beside him, Boyce turned a page of his notebook and waited for Webb's reply, but he only shrugged as if admitting that piece of bad luck.

'And that made you decide to clear out?' Finch continued. 'When exactly did you make a run for it?'

'Early Sunday morning. It seemed better than going Saturday night. I'd only got a couple of quid on me and I thought there'd be less chance of you lot hanging about Nina's first thing on a Sunday morning. I was going to borrow some money off her. Anyway, you turned up so I had to leave. I spent the day in an empty barn and went back after dark. It was Nina's idea I stayed the night and left this morning. She said if I caught the bus to Millstead I could pick up the London coach from there. Before I left, she gave me a letter for Zoe Hamilton, Max's ex-wife.' His face darkened, the expression changing from adolescent appeal to childish outrage and fury. 'Nina said she'd put me up for a few days but instead the bloody bitch turned me in.'

Finch ignored both the outburst and Danny's insistence on the part Nina had played in helping him escape to London, a quite deliberate attempt to exonerate himself and lay as much of the blame on her as he could. His face expressionless, he merely said,

'I'd like to return to Friday morning, Mr Webb. We shall need a full account of your movements between nine o'clock and twelve thirty.'

Webb replied quickly, 'I stayed in bed until about ten o'clock.'

'Any witnesses?' Finch asked.

'I didn't have a woman shacked up with me, if that's what you mean.'

Danny spoke with something of his old swagger in an attempt to brazen it out.

'I wasn't thinking of that,' Finch replied equably. 'I meant Mr Burnett.'

'No, I don't think Lionel saw me. When I left, I walked down the drive past the cottage but he didn't come out. I wasn't all that keen, anyway, on seeing him. I knew bloody well he'd stop me and make a fuss about the caravan. He'd already had a whinge about the rubbish I'd left at the bottom of the steps.'

'Mr Burnett was at home?' Finch slipped the question in casually.

'I suppose so,' Danny said indifferently. 'His car was in the drive.'

'I see. And where did you go when you left the caravan?'

'I went to the Feathers for a drink.'

'No, you didn't, Mr Webb; or, at least, not until half past eleven. We've already checked that with the landlord.'

'Oh, Christ,' Danny said softly. He was silent for several seconds, his head lowered so that Finch could see only the top of his head with its thinning, fine brown hair. When he raised it, his face had again assumed the expression of ashamed entreaty and he sought for Finch's eyes, looking straight into them. It was easy to see why Nina Gifford had supported him all those years. Even if one discounted the blood-tie between them, Danny had the gift of appealing to one's sympathy, of creating the image of the innocent whom no one understood and whom life had treated unfairly. With his thin, boyish features and air of hurt, bewildered honesty, he looked the part.

'You're not going to believe this,' he began.

'Try me,' Finch suggested cheerfully.

'I went to look round the church in the village. God knows why; I can't explain. I haven't been in a church for years; not since I left home. But I suddenly wanted to have a look inside one again. For old time's sake, perhaps.'

He gave Finch a small, lop-sided smile, inviting his amusement and his credence.

'Did anyone see you?' Finch asked, his own face expressionless.

'No, I don't think so. If you've been down to the village, you'll know it's not in the centre. It's between Lionel's house and the others. There's a couple of cottages opposite but that's all. I didn't see anyone about and the church itself was empty.'

It was a perfectly accurate description of the siting of the church in Althorpe, but one which Danny could have discovered at almost any time during his stay in the village.

'And how long were you there?' Finch asked.

'About an hour, I suppose. I wandered about for a while and then sat in the porch while I had a cigarette. Then I walked back to the Feathers.'

The timing fitted, too, but also proved nothing. Danny could have easily worked out how long it would take him to walk from the cottage to the church and back to the Feathers, allowing roughly the right length of time he had stayed in the building.

Finch rose to his feet, Danny following him with his eyes.

'What's happening now?' he asked, his voice sharp with anxiety.

'You'll be held,' Finch said simply and saw the innocent, hard-done-by expression turn to one of fear.

'On what grounds, for Christ's sake? You're not going to charge me, are you? I've told you, I had nothing to do with Quinn's murder! Why the hell should I want to kill him? I'd only met him once . . .'

'You'll be held pending further inquiries,' Finch continued, raising his voice, and nodded to Boyce, who put away his notebook. The two men left the room, the constable, who had been waiting outside, resuming his position just inside the door.

'We'll get him back to headquarters,' Finch told the sergeant as they stood outside in the corridor. 'I'll have a word with Blakeny and arrange for Webb to be kept here until Marsh and one of the others can be sent over to pick him up. Now we've found Webb, we shan't need them on the search.'

'What about getting him to make a statement?'

'We'll do that later when he's back on our patch.'

'Do you reckon he's guilty?'

'I don't know,' Finch confessed. 'He's got no alibi or, at least, not one that any witnesses can verify, so he could have killed Quinn. It wouldn't have taken him long to get from the caravan to the Giffords' place, especially if he cut across the fields. But, as he himself said, and quite rightly, too, in my opinion, why should he want to kill Quinn?'

'Unless Nina Gifford was right,' Boyce put in.

'How?' Finch asked sharply.

'Don't you remember her theory that Quinn was killed by an intruder? We discussed it at the time and didn't think it was very likely. But suppose Webb got into the house and Quinn found him in the act of helping himself to some of Max Gifford's sketches? Quinn may have threatened to tell Nina so Webb clobbered him.'

As a theory, it had a certain appeal which Finch couldn't deny. It fitted in neatly with what they already knew of Webb's past dealings with Quinn over Gifford's drawings, with the added motivation that if Danny Webb had learned from Lionel Burnett of the proposed exhibition, anything by Gifford would have increased in value and would therefore be worth getting hold of by almost any means. But, all the same, it was flawed.

'Max Gifford would have heard them quarrelling,' Finch pointed out. 'His portfolios of drawings are kept in the dining-room and that opens off the hall. Any noise would have gone straight up the stairs.'

'All right, then. So Webb suggests to Quinn they go somewhere else to discuss it and he either kills him in the kitchen or in the yard.'

'Could be,' Finch agreed doubtfully. He still wasn't convinced. 'All the same, I can't see Webb being sufficiently frightened by Quinn's threat to tell his sister that he'd murder him.'

'Why not?'

'Because as far as she was concerned, it wouldn't have made any difference.'

'But did Webb know that?'

'Oh, yes.' Finch was quite positive. 'Webb knows it. And she knows it. Don't you see, Tom, it's what keeps them together? It's a conspiracy of dependence. Take Nina Gifford away and Webb would collapse like a heap of old clothes. But the reverse is also true. Without him, she's just as lost.'

He might have added but didn't that, as a relationship, it was even more binding than that between Nina and Max. The loss of Max would leave a huge gap in her life which time would slowly fill. But nothing would bridge the chasm that Danny would leave behind.

As they talked, they had been walking towards the entrance, where they both paused.

'So what happens now?' Boyce asked, though Finch could tell by his hang-dog look that the sergeant was very well aware what the answer would be.

'You go on checking down those lists for Quinn's partner,' Finch said, pretending as he looked at his watch not to see the sergeant's long-suffering expression.

'And you?'

'I'll phone headquarters from here and get Marsh and Simpson organised to pick up Danny Webb. After that, there should be just about enough time to drive over to Heversham and interview Danny's father and aunt. Old Mr Webb's retired now, so I'll have to get his exact address from Danny before I go. It's worth the trip, I think. There may be some old gossip worth raking up over there.' He said it wryly, remembering Blanche Lester's comment on his methods of investigation.

'First of all, though, I'll have a word with Blakeny.'

'See you then,' Boyce replied, setting off down the steps.

As he reached the bottom, Finch called after him on a sudden impulse.

'Yes, what is it?' Boyce asked, turning to look back.

'Check Bruce Lawford this afternoon, will you? He's on your list.'

The sergeant seemed about to query the request but Finch, anticipating his curiosity, had already retreated inside the building. It might be tempting fate to pick out that one particular name from among the others, but the Chief Inspector had no intention of provoking it still further by trying to explain his reasons.

14

Finch left London just after half past three, taking the M11 to Cambridge and turning off at Bishops Stortford. Once clear of the city, he was able to make good time and it was getting on for five o'clock when he approached the outskirts of Heversham down a minor road that dipped and swung through the scattered villages of rural Essex.

Its centre was small and nuclear, a collection of houses and cottages grouped round the church beside which stood the rectory, Nina Gifford's former home, not dissimilar to Althorpe House in its heavy, Victorian solidity and dense shrubbery which isolated it from the surrounding buildings. Even the church stood aloof, as if keeping itself apart from the everyday life of the people it served.

The dependence of the place on agriculture was everywhere apparent. The farm-land crowded down to the backs of the houses so that, beyond them and their little garden plots, hedged in with quickthorn, one could see the cultivated fields of sugar beet, wheat and potatoes and, beyond those on the left, the barns and silos of a farm which stood out above the level view. Between some of the houses, five-barred gates gave access to the land and, as Finch entered the village, he was forced to slow down behind a tractor which occupied the width of the road until it turned off through an open gateway beside the Parish Hall.

Opposite it was the house for which he was looking: Ivy Place, a small, detached, brick and slate building, its front façade entirely covered by the creeper from which it had doubtlessly derived its name and through which four sash windows and a central door appeared to have been cut out. The effect was oddly sinister for, across the windows and door frame, little unpruned tendrils were beginning to creep as if the ivy were only waiting its opportunity to take the house over completely, winding its way into rooms and up the staircase until the whole building was occupied with leaves. The twisted trunks from which the ivy grew close to the front wall were as thick as Finch's arm and covered with a coarse, hairy growth which seemed to emphasise its crudely vigorous vegetable life. As he walked up the path to the front door, he imagined the roots spreading with the same insidious energy beneath the foundations as its branches scrambled up the brickwork.

There was a black iron ring which he banged and presently the door was opened by a tall, thin, elderly woman, dressed in a black skirt and dark-patterned blouse, her grey hair scraped back into a small bun, who demanded abruptly to know what his business was. Finch produced his card, explaining that he was making official police inquiries, and he was somewhat grudgingly invited to step inside the hall, although he was allowed no further than the coconut-fibre doormat.

'Inquiries into what?' she demanded.

'Your nephew, Daniel Webb,' Finch replied. She reminded him of a formidable primary school teacher in whose class he had once spent a terrified year at the age of eight and who had cracked him over the knuckles with a ruler for not knowing his nine times table. 'I believe I'm right in thinking you're his aunt, Miss Webb?'

'I am.' Miss Webb acknowledged the relationship as reluctantly as she had invited him into the house. 'Is Daniel in some trouble with the police?'

'I'm afraid so.'

She made no comment as she returned his card to him, as if his announcement came as no surprise to her, merely remarking, 'Then you'd better come this way,' before leading him down the passage to a door at the far end which she opened, adding over her shoulder, 'My brother is very deaf. I would prefer you discussed this matter with me.'

The room that they entered was small and crowded with dark, heavy furniture which Finch assumed they had brought with them from the more spacious rectory on the Reverend Webb's retirement. It was good, solid, well-made stuff, polished to a high gloss, but much too overpowering for the limited accommodation. The patterned carpet and dark red wallpaper added their own claustrophobic atmosphere so that the air itself appeared squeezed out and there seemed no space for mere people, certainly not for the frail, elderly man who was seated by the window in a high-backed armchair, a rug over his knees on which two fragile hands, trembling continuously, lay like pale leaves blown in from some forlorn winter garden. He seemed barricaded in with furniture, the long, heavy curtains forming a palisade on one side, a table containing medicine bottles on the other, while in front of him stood a footstool on which rested two long, thin feet clad in carpet slippers.

Max Gifford, too, was an old man but, compared to Mr Webb, he was alive and vigorous. He had preserved his intelligence and personality, a sense of presence. Nina Gifford's father seemed no more than a bundle of clothes propped up in a corner, surmounted by a head from which most of the flesh had shrunk away leaving only the bony protuberances of nose, chin and forehead and the dark, fallen orifices of eyes and mouth. The eyes turned to Finch as he entered the room but showed no sign of curiosity. They were merely registering his presence.

'It's someone called about Daniel,' Miss Webb announced, leaning over him and raising her voice.

'Daniel?' the old man repeated.

'He doesn't remember,' she continued, turning to Finch. 'Sit down.'

She indicated the other high-backed chair which stood on the far side of the window, drawing up for herself a straight chair from the central table and turning it round to face him.

'Well?' she said, taking her own seat.

Finch lowered himself into the armchair. Now that he had both the Webbs in view, brother and sister, he could see a family likeness. They were out of the same mould – tall, thin, long-faced, humourless, with too much forehead and a sparsity of flesh and hair, as if these were extravagances of nature which one could well do without. He could see also that Danny had inherited their physical features; their stubbornness and lack of humour, too. It was probably these shared characteristics which had caused friction in his childhood and had finally driven him away. But it must have been the dissimilarities which had forced Nina to leave home. Stifled by its atmosphere, she would have welcomed the chance to escape which Max Gifford with his vigour and his relaxed life-style had offered her.

'I'm investigating a case of possible fraud in which your nephew might be implicated,' Finch explained. The word 'murder' seemed too shocking to use in front of these two elderly people.

'I see,' said Miss Webb grimly, folding her lips.

'I came to see you because I need to know a little more about Daniel's background. A report has to be made, you see.'

To his relief, she seemed to accept this inadequate and deliberately vague explanation for she remarked disapprovingly, 'I suppose it's become fashionable these days for social factors to be taken into consideration; a great mistake, in my opinion, and a contributory factor in the increasing crime rate. Anyone who breaks the law should be made to face up to the consequences of their behaviour, not excused. I am surprised the police have become party to it.' Finch made a deprecatory gesture with his hand which she ignored. 'As far as Daniel is concerned, there is very little I can say in his defence. He was brought up in a Christian household in which strict standards were always maintained. My brother and I both did our best to instil in him a correct moral attitude, but it wasn't easy. He was always wilful and disobedient, even as a small child, with very little sense of responsibility. At school it was exactly the same. He was always in trouble. In fact, the headmaster refused to allow him to stay on into the sixth form as he felt Daniel's academic record was too poor and he would be an undesirable influence on the other boys.'

She spoke without emotion, as if the condemnation had been rehearsed, and Finch suspected that, over the years, it had become a set speech which she repeated whenever Daniel's character was called into question.

'What did he do when he left school?' Finch asked.

'He had several jobs, none of which lasted very long. He also made some quite unsuitable friends whom he used to bring home. In the end, his father and I refused to tolerate it any longer and he was told to choose. After all, my brother was at the time still rector of the parish and had his own position and standing to consider. Neither could I be expected to have young men and women arriving at all hours, sometimes the worse for drink, and turning the house into a beer-garden.'

Remembering the state of Lionel Burnett's caravan, Finch could almost sympathise with her. The choice which Danny had made was inevitable but all the same he wanted to hear her reply.

'And he chose to go?'

'He was eighteen.' Miss Webb sounded defensive and Finch wondered if, in her more honest moments, she might not have considered how far she herself was responsible for what Danny had become. 'He was legally of age. One of his friends had just obtained a job in London and Daniel went with him. I believe there was talk of sharing a flat, but I don't think the arrangement lasted very long.'

'Did he keep in touch?'

'Very infrequently, and only then when he was short of money. After his father retired, I wrote to Daniel explaining that, as we were now living on his pension, it would no longer be possible for us to support him if he got into financial difficulties. After that, the letters and visits virtually stopped.'

At this point, old Mr Webb, who had appeared not to be taking any notice of either Finch or the conversation but had remained silent, staring out through the window at a small, enclosed back garden, turned towards them and asked in a high, trembling voice, 'Daniel? Has Daniel come?'

Miss Webb rose from her chair to bend over him.

'No, Henry,' she said loudly. 'It's someone asking about Daniel, that's all.'

The old man appeared not to understand what she was saying, for he continued, 'He ought to be home soon.'

'One of these days, perhaps, Henry. But he went away to London. Don't you remember?'

Miss Webb's tone became more insistent, with the edge of some other quality about it that Finch could not quite define. It was not exactly triumph; for all her faults, she had too much Christian charity for that, but it was the voice of a woman who believed the truth must always be spoken, whatever the circumstances, and who found a self-righteous satisfaction in doing so.

Mr Webb fell silent and his sister tidied him up before returning to her chair, rearranging the rug over his knees and placing his hands side by side on top of it in much the same manner, Finch imagined, that she would move the ornaments along the mantelshelf into their precise positions.

'He kept in touch with his sister, Nina,' Finch remarked when she had resumed her seat. He made the comment casually but watched her face closely as he said it and saw two patches of dull red appear on her cheekbones. Although she might be capable of discussing Danny almost neutrally, as if she had learned to come to terms with his shortcomings and misdemeanours, it was quite clear that Nina could still arouse some old, emotional response.

'That doesn't surprise me in the least,' she replied, a harder snap in her voice. 'That girl always had the worst possible influence over Daniel. I blame her for much that went wrong. She seemed to go out of her way to undermine my authority over him. Being older than he was, she should have known better. Half of the mischief he was involved in was instigated by her. In fact, I'm not sure that Daniel's decision to leave home wasn't largely her fault. After he left, we found some letters she had sent him through a school friend, full of descriptions of parties she had been to and public houses she had visited; what she called "having a good time". She was quite lacking in any sense of responsibility.'

'Her running away from home must have had some effect on him,' Finch said with an innocent expression.

'We tried to keep the truth from him, of course, but there was so much gossip in the village that I'm afraid he found out what had happened from other people. It broke Henry's heart. She simply walked out early one morning with a suitcase, leaving a note on the dining-room table.'

It was a small point but interesting all the same, and Finch wondered if Danny hadn't been subconsciously following her example when he, too, chose to clear out of the caravan in the early hours of the morning.

'Wasn't she under age?' Finch asked. They had at last got to the subject of Nina Gifford, a topic he intended following through as far as Miss Webb would allow him.

'She was seventeen. I felt the police should have been informed. After all, the man was years older than her and a total stranger.'

'You never met him?'

'No. I believe he was from London. She said very little about him in her letter. The whole business was a madness! Total folly!'

'And were the police called in?'

'No. Henry refused to allow it. "Let her go," he said. "But I never want her name mentioned in this house again."'

It was an embargo which still seemed to be in operation, for

Finch realised that Miss Webb had never once referred to her niece by name. Nor did she, even when speaking of her brother, so much as glance in his direction, as if the senile old man occupying the chair by the window had no connection with the Reverend Henry Webb who had been involved in that family drama all those years before.

'The fact was,' Miss Webb continued, 'we had already had dealings with the police only a short time before and Henry felt there had been enough trouble in the village without stirring up another scandal.'

'Scandal?' Finch picked the word up eagerly, wondering if this might not concern the facts about Nina's past about which Quinn had been so curious. 'To do with your niece?'

'Oh, no!' Miss Webb was quick to put him right. 'The church was broken into and the altar desecrated. Of course, the police had to be informed and inquiries were made round the village which caused a lot of ill-feeling. Henry had his suspicions, you see, of the people who were involved, although he didn't like to name them.'

She broke off and got to her feet once again, this time to go to the sideboard, a drawer of which she opened and took from it a small, black-painted, metal cash-box, shielding it from old Mr Webb's sight as she carried it back to her chair, although her caution seemed unnecessary. He had withdrawn once more into indifference and was staring out again through the window.

Finch watched her curiously as she lifted the lid of the box. It was full of papers – letters mostly, still in their original envelopes, and Finch suspected that they were those sent by Danny over the years; possibly Nina's farewell message was also among them, preserved not as a love keepsake as Lionel Burnett had saved the scrawled notes she had sent him, but as proof of betrayal and disaffection, a black museum of the emotions. Among them were several newspaper cuttings, one of which Miss Webb, with another of her surreptitious glances at her brother, passed to Finch. It was from the *Daily Telegraph* for 8 June 1953 and had as its headline, 'Vicar's Pulpit Appeal.'

The story itself was short and factual, merely stating that, following the desecration of his church, St Michael's in Heversham, Essex, the Reverend Henry Webb had appealed to his parishioners to assist the police in their inquiries. 'You must not allow family loyalties to protect those guilty of the sin of sacrilege,' he had said. The report concluded with the statement that two youths were helping the police with their inquiries.

Finch returned the cutting, at a loss to know why Miss Webb had shown it to him. Her motive was not long in making itself clear.

'Henry already had this trouble on his hands,' she said, pinching in her lips. 'The village was full of journalists, taking photographs; even reports in some of the less reputable newspapers of black-magic rites; absolute nonsense, of course. The two boys concerned were simply local delinquents who knew no better than to break into the church and vandalise the altar. Naturally, it caused a great number of problems for Henry: meetings with the Parish Council and the bishop, who had to reconsecrate the church, discussions with the boys' parents and probation officers. I'm afraid neither Henry nor I had time to notice what *she* was up to. It was only afterwards that we realised she had been slipping away to meet that man.'

'Max Gifford?' Finch suggested in his blandest tone. It seemed time that his name, at least, should be mentioned.

Miss Webb carefully refolded the cutting and returned it to the box tucking it away and, as she did so, allowing Finch a glimpse of a corner of a sheet of white paper which obtruded above the other contents.

'I don't know his name,' she replied, 'and I have no desire to know it. I hold him responsible for what happened. He was staying in the next village, it seems, at the Rose and Crown, and had walked over here one Saturday afternoon. They met. At least, I am repeating hearsay which was told to me later by local people who, under the guise of being helpful, took pleasure in passing on the gossip to Henry and myself. Several of Henry's parishioners saw them together, but didn't think it important enough at the time to mention the fact either to me or to her father until it was too late. She had evidently been meeting him half-way between the two villages, going off on her bicycle and making the excuse that she was spending the evening with a school friend. Her deception was quite cleverly planned. She even asked the friend to come to the house to collect her on one or two occasions so that we wouldn't be suspicious. She is totally amoral.'

It was no doubt part of her self-protection which she had built up over the years that made her unaware of the implied hostility of the local people that lay behind much of what she had told him. Even the incident of the desecration of the church, seized on so eagerly by the newspapers, especially with its undercurrent of possible black-magic ritual, could have been motivated as much by a desire to get back at the vicar and his sister as by a simple urge to vandalise. And yet this possibility appeared not to have crossed her mind, any more than the thought that she and her brother might have been in any way to blame for what Nina and Danny had done. Her self-righteousness was like armour.

'"Amoral"?' Finch picked up the word. It was an aspect of Nina Gifford which he himself had been aware of, but not in the sense in which Miss Webb was using the term. Nina Gifford had her own set of moral values which an older generation of people, certainly her aunt and her father, would discount as unworthy by normal codes of behaviour. But Nina's were not circumscribed by accepted mores. Hers were based on the needs of those she loved. So she would lie and cheat and possibly steal, perhaps even commit murder, not out of confirmed wickedness but only when survival, hers or those she cared for, depended on it.

'Like her mother!' Miss Webb said, her voice so loud that it penetrated even old Mr Webb's consciousness, for he turned from his vacant survey of the garden to look at her, his face troubled. But Miss Webb had gone beyond the point of caring. The bitterness which she had carried for nearly fifty years had, at last, found expression. 'God knows why he married her. She was a farmer's daughter, years younger than him; not even properly educated; certainly not suitable for a vicar's wife. They'd been married for less than a year when she ran off and left him.'

'But she came back?'

'Oh, yes, but only because her mother was dying. Henry forgave her and the marriage was patched up somehow. It meant moving to another parish, of course. He could hardly remain in the same district with everyone gossiping behind his back. But that's the kind of blood that Nina and Danny inherited. It's no wonder with her as an example that they turned out the way they did.'

To Finch's relief, the outburst was cut short by a little cry from old Mr Webb, who had been watching their faces with the staring intensity of the deaf. It was unlikely that he had followed their conversation. His expression suggested that, like a child, he had grasped only the emotions and these had frightened him. He was struggling to rise from his chair, pushing back the folds of the blanket with his frail hands.

'Where are they, Connie?' he was asking. 'They should be home by now. Where have they gone to?'

Miss Webb went to him immediately, soothing, tucking, tidying, her rigid back bent solicitously over him.

While she was so occupied, Finch rose to his feet and, using his body to hide the box in much the same way as she had done, flicked back the lid and drew out the sheet of paper so that half of it was visible. There was no need for him to see more. What it contained was obvious to him and, his face perfectly bland, he pushed it back again among the other contents and quietly reclosed the lid.

'I'll let myself out,' he said, but he doubted if she heard him. As he left the room he could hear her voice raised in explanation, although perhaps admonition might have better described it.

'They've left home, Henry. They went away a long time ago. They won't be coming back.'

She might, he thought savagely, as he shut the front door

behind him and walked away from the house, have found it in her heart to spare the old man that final truth.

Boyce was waiting for him when he returned to the office.

'Webb's downstairs,' he announced as soon as Finch entered the room. 'Marsh and Simpson brought him back a couple of hours ago. I suppose you'll want me to hang on here while you get a statement out of him.'

He seemed filled with gloom at the prospect, which had obviously occupied his mind since his return from London, for until Finch reminded him he appeared to have forgotten the purpose of his trip.

'That can wait,' Finch told him. 'How did you get on this afternoon? Did you see Bruce Lawford?'

'Oh, him. No, as a matter of fact, I didn't. He's out of the country, filming. I had a word with his secretary but she wasn't much help. All she could tell me was that Lawford and Quinn met for lunch some time in February at Quinn's suggestion; she didn't know what about and she hadn't heard anything about a partnership. Nor had any of the others I talked to, come to that.'

'Filming?' Finch repeated.

'That's right. He's a television producer. He's working on some serial at the moment, set partly in Spain, so he's over in Madrid. Nice work if you can get it, eh? I wouldn't mind a few weeks in the sun, all expenses paid, too. The most I'll manage this year is a couple of weeks in Cornwall if I'm lucky.'

Finch hardly heard him. The familiarity of the name now made sense to him. When he had first seen it on Miss Martin's list, he had associated it with the printed word and had made the assumption that he must have read it in a newspaper. Now he realized that he had been wrong in that conclusion. He had seen it on the credit titles of a television play that he had watched a couple of months before. Its title now escaped him and all that remained in his mind were images of the sea, beautifully photographed, and a death by drowning so powerful in its realism that he had looked out for the name of the producer at the end.

He was not normally a television enthusiast, rarely having time to watch, and only then when he was too tired to do anything more demanding than sit in front of the screen. Quite frequently he fell asleep in the middle of a programme, waking to find that the news had been replaced by some imported American detective serial so that, for a few bewildered seconds, it appeared that a high-speed car-chase or a rooftop shoot-out were occupying the main nine o'clock headlines. Not that it would have been all that surprising if it had. Quite often the real world had the unpleasant and disturbing tendency to reflect the imagined, so that one was not sure which mirror with the ugly, distorting twist of violence running across its surface was being held up to the world.

'That programme a few weeks ago,' he began.

'What programme?' Boyce demanded. He had been in the middle of complaining that even Cornwall might be out of the question next summer, as the gearbox on the car would probably need replacing and there was no way he could afford both.

'At the end of March. Bruce Lawford produced it.'

'Who was in it?' Boyce asked, which was no help at all.

'That tall actor with the moustache.'

'Do you mean Maurice Davies? He's in *Shades of Night* on ATV on a Thursday evening.'

'How should I know?' Finch demanded irritably. It was like trying to explain a complicated route to someone who was a stranger in the district, when familiar landmarks become totally meaningless and one is forced to describe features of an area which one hadn't oneself looked at properly for years. 'All I know is it was set on an island off the coast of Scotland and the man was drowned trying to get back.'

'Oh, I know which one you mean.' Boyce sounded relieved at having got there at last. 'It was called something like "Farewell to Summer". The chap was a game-warden, wasn't he? Something to do with wild-life, anyway. Then his wife decided she'd had enough and caught the steamer back to civilisation. He had a few bevvies in the meantime, realised a woman was better than an island full of bloody gannets and tried to join her. His boat went arse over tip half-way across.'

It was a travesty of the plot, but it hardly mattered. They were clearly talking about the same play.

'As a matter of fact,' Boyce continued, 'wasn't it one of those semi-documentaries based on a real-life story? I seem to remember there was a bit of a fuss in the *Express* the next day, saying if the writer and producer wanted to make a programme about the bloke, they should stick to the facts and not muck about with them.'

'My God!' Finch said softly. 'That's the answer.'

Boyce looked at him.

'What answer?'

'To Quinn's murder. The facts, Tom! You know, like in the play? They've been staring me in the face, some of them for the past few days, and I haven't had the gumption to put them together to make the right story.'

As he said it, he remembered the feeling he had experienced when talking to Blanche Lester in the park about Nina Gifford's relationship with Max, and how the details had become connected in his mind with memories of the fairy-story he had heard in school of the princess and the wicked fairy godmother.

'What facts are you talking about?' Boyce was asking. 'If you mean evidence, we've gone over that enough times, God help us. I don't see how you can rearrange any of it. And what's this about a story, anyway? We're not dealing with a television plot, you know.'

'Of course we're not, and that's the whole point. It's real; there's nothing fictional about it. So let's take another look at that real evidence which we haven't so far been able to fit into a theory. Fact number one: someone, presumably the murderer, wiped the floor with a sack after Quinn's body had been dumped in the outhouse. Fact number two: Gifford divorced his first wife in 1937, but he and Nina never married. Fact number three, and I've only discovered this piece of evidence this afternoon and it didn't mean anything to me at the time: the church at Heversham was broken into in 1953 and the altar was desecrated. It made quite a stir at the time, enough to get into some of the London dailies.'

'I don't get the connection,' Boyce said heavily.

'No?' said Finch. 'Then I'll tell you. There's something else I found out this afternoon, too, which put me on to it. Added together it gives Quinn's murderer a motive, something we haven't so far been able to establish.'

He made the account as brief as he could, aware that time was passing and that, before the arrest could be made, there were still a few facts he had to check with Danny Webb.

Webb parted with the information reluctantly. He had been brought up from the cells into an interview room, which he entered with the same look of eager appeal which now seemed his habitual expression, rather than the air of surly insolence with which he had first greeted the Chief Inspector. A few hours in custody had cut him down to size. In his time, Finch had known hundreds of Danny Webbs. Small-time crooks and petty thieves, they usually ended up at the bottom of the heap; lost, pathetic, lonely men, beaten by the system which they had once, with the arrogance of youth, imagined they could manipulate. Danny Webb was already half-way down that road.

He answered Finch's questions with an air of bewilderment.

'What the hell's it all about?' he asked when the Chief Inspector had finished.

Finch didn't even bother to reply. He grasped Boyce's shoulder as they made for the door, half-pushing him through it, at the same time thrusting his other arm into the sleeve of his raincoat. He was still putting it on when they emerged from the building into the car-park.

Waiting while Boyce unlocked the car, he allowed himself a few moments' grace to look up at the sky.

It was already twilight, though a dull ember of light still faintly charred the darkness to the west where the sun, slipping down beyond the horizon's rim, cast up a cindery incandescence.

By the time they reached Althorpe House, the glimmer had vanished and night had taken over; proper darkness, not the bastard city dusk which is never entirely complete but is always tinged with the red glow of lights shining upwards and tinselled with the cheap jewellery of the street-lamps. The stars were out and the sky was vast; against it the bulk of Althorpe House seemed larger than usual, square, massive, safe, its chimney stacks blocks of solid blackness. There was no light showing in the front windows, only a dark sheen on glass.

At Finch's instructions, Boyce parked just inside the gate and they approached the house on foot, following the pale curve of the gravelled drive round to the back.

At the yard entrance, Finch stopped abruptly, overwhelmed by a feeling of déjà vu which, with its sudden, unexpected jarring of all normal responses, heightens awareness and sharpens the senses to a pitch beyond common, everyday perception.

The yard stretched out in front of him, enclosed on two sides by buildings; on his left, the house itself, soaring upwards like a cliff of brick; to his right, the lower escarpment of the outhouses, the irregular peak of their roofs cutting the sky into a triangle. Between them, the floor of the yard had vanished into the darkness, so that he had the impression of standing on the edge of a huge, rectangular tank filled with black water across which he must plunge towards the square of lighted window which, with its curtains drawn, glowed with a subdued, yellowish gleam and seemed to symbolise old, half-forgotten pleasures: firelight, and lamplight shining down onto a white tablecloth set with cups and plates.

While his attention was centred on the window and the black gulf which separated him from it, he was aware at the same time of the night-noises which surrounded him: the furtive shuffling of some creature in the bushes, the tinkling rustle of the ivy which grew up the wall at his side, the rasp of branch on branch and, further away still, the subdued tumult of a light wind in the trees, sounding like some far-off, landlocked sea beating on a distant shore.

And beyond that, silence and darkness which only the stars inhabited.

Coming home. The phrase came into his mind simultaneously with all the other sensations and, in the same split second of time, banished them. The connection had been made and his rational mind took over. He was no longer the child pausing in the backyard to savour the moment of home-coming. There was no table laid for tea or Children's Hour on the wireless; no fire banked so high in the kitchen range that it stung the skin to sit near it; no oil-lamp, although conscious memory could recreate its milky glass globe and polished brass base, the circular pool of light it cast on the white tablecloth and his scattered schoolbooks.

He was a middle-aged Inspector of Police, halting momentarily at the entrance to the yard of Althorpe House as if accustoming his eyes to the darkness, and behind the lighted window the only person who waited for him was Nina Gifford.

15

After leaving Danny at the bus-stop, Nina walked home across the fields. The countryside had lost its early morning beauty and had settled down into the mere ordinariness of the familiar landscape, untransformed, unglorified. Without Danny, the rest of the day also assumed the same humdrum monotony. She woke Max and gave him his breakfast, got him washed and settled back into bed. He seemed disinclined to talk and she made no efforts herself to force conversation.

Downstairs, she cleared the bedding from the sofa and put it away, unable to bear this reminder of Danny's presence, and once she had washed up his breakfast things there was nothing left of him except her own sense of bereavement, although she tried to follow him in her imagination, checking the kitchen clock every so often to relate his time to hers. Ten forty-five and he'd be arriving in Victoria. Eleven twenty and he should be on his way to Zoe's, if not actually there. She tried to picture him walking along the North End Road to Zoe's turning, finding the number of the house and descending the basement steps.

Her imagination broke down after that. She couldn't envisage what sort of welcome Zoe would give him or how Danny would behave in that dark, little underground room, and she wished to hell Zoe was on the phone so that she could ring up and talk to him, if only to reiterate the warning that he had not given her time to repeat before they parted that morning.

At lunch-time, however, the pattern was broken. Max suddenly announced that he wanted to get up.

'Now?' she asked, astonished, her attention focusing on him properly for the first time that day. She saw at once that he looked better; still not quite his former self but at least not the grey-faced, exhausted old man who had lain so listlessly in bed for the past few days.

'Yes, I'm fed up with lying here, Nine. That bloody cedar tree is getting on my nerves. If it isn't staring in at me through the window during the day, it's fidgeting about muttering to itself half the night. I want a change of scene.'

'All right,' she conceded. 'But eat your lunch first.'

He insisted on dressing himself or, at least, putting on as many of his clothes as he could manage alone. Sent outside to wait on the landing, Nina watched him through the crack of the door which she had deliberately left ajar, marvelling at his persistence as he struggled into his shirt and hoisted himself painfully up from the bed to drag his trousers over his backside. It was as much as she could do not to burst in and help him. Finally, when he had transferred his cigarettes and matches from the bedside table to his pocket, he called out to her, his face proud at his achievement, while she knelt at his feet like a disciple, she thought with a mixture of genuine admiration and amused irreverence, to put on his socks and shoes.

'There!' she said, patting his ankle as she tied the last lace.

Getting him downstairs took all of ten minutes. They halted at every tread, Max carefully realigning his feet before tentatively feeling for the next one. At the bottom he paused, clinging to the newel-post, a curious, far-away expression on his face, as if all his concentration were turned inwards in the effort of gathering up sufficient strength for the final trek into the kitchen. They made it at last and she lowered him into the basket chair which she placed in its habitual position near the back door.

'Brandy?' she asked him. He oughtn't to drink, of course, but it would be hours before he took his tablets and she felt some celebration was called for. Fetching the bottle, she realised how little was left. She and Danny had almost finished it the previous evening.

He sipped it leisurely, holding the glass between both his hands as if drawing up the essence of the spirit through its sides, his face turned towards the sun to absorb its warmth with the same, slow, pleasurable indulgence of the senses.

Later, he slept, waking when she walked past him to close the back door, the sun having moved down behind the house, leaving the yard in shadow.

'What's the time, Nina?' he asked.

'Nearly quarter past seven.'

He had slept longer than usual, exhausted, no doubt, by the exertion of dressing and coming downstairs.

'I can smell something cooking.'

'It's supper.'

While he had been asleep, she had prepared the evening meal, kidneys in gravy, because that was all the village shop had to offer in the way of meat that had looked at all appetising. Besides, she had an almost superstitious belief in the efficacy of offal as nourishment for the body; liver, brains, heart, they did you more good than the usual stewing steak or chops. They were cheaper, too, which was another consideration almost as important.

She took the casserole dish out of the oven to show him, lifting the lid to reveal them sizzling in their rich juices, the slices of onion reduced to a glorious, pulpy mass of pure flavour.

'It looks good,' he said appreciatively.

'It is good,' she retorted.

She was suddenly happy that he was at last showing an interest in food. He was her old Max again. The intervening days were like a dark valley out of which they had both begun slowly to climb.

'Tell you what,' Max was saying. 'What about a bottle of something to go with it? Like the old times in the studio, eh, Nine?'

She knew what he meant. In fact, for a few seconds, she felt they shared the same memory: the big, upper room, with the scarred, circular table they had bought in a second-hand shop in Pimlico standing under the window, half-laid for supper with the long French loaf and the bottle of wine. Max had painted it once, one of the few still-lifes he had ever attempted. It was still hanging in the sitting-room because no one had wanted to buy it and even she had to admit that it wasn't his best work; he had never been inspired by mere objects. Even so, he had caught something of their amplitude and their promise of good living in the rough, crisp crust of the bread and the light glistening richly on the shoulders of the dark wine-bottle.

All the same, she hesitated, thinking about the cost. But Max, as if anticipating her doubt, was fumbling in his pocket and producing a five-pound note. God knows where he had got it from. Judging by its crumpled condition, he must have been hanging on to it for months.

'Go on, Nine,' he coaxed. 'Even the Feathers ought to be able to rustle up a bottle of plonk.'

She got her bike out of the stable and set off down the drive. The sun was setting, but she thought she ought to be back before dark; a minor consideration, but one that worried her slightly nevertheless. Since Max had become crippled, she so rarely went out in the evenings that the batteries in the lamps must have long since corroded.

All the lights were on in the Feathers, including the red-shaded wall-lamps in the shape of candles and the pink strip-light over the bar. It seemed strange to plunge into that pink and red glow when outside the sky was still on fire with the real scarlet and gold of the setting sun. She could see it through one of the tiny casement windows, like a bonfire on the far side of the wheatfield across the road, and, in the distance, a line of trees cut out in dark silhouette against it. It was the sort of view she liked, dramatic and colourful. Not to Max's taste, though. That's chocolate-box stuff, he would have said. He hated snow for the same reason. Christmas cards had ruined it for him.

The bar was almost empty; it was still too early for the real evening trade. There were only two men at the counter, farm-hands having a pint on their way home, she imagined. Their bikes had been propped up outside. She knew only one of the men by sight. He'd called at the house once for water when his tractor had boiled over and they had stood talking in the yard for a while about the previous owners. Nina had listened reluctantly. She had preferred not to know who had inhabited the place before she and Max moved in. Now, not remembering his name, she nodded to him and he nodded back, having also forgotten hers, and, moving his beer mug along the counter to make room for her, began talking in a low voice to his companion, half-turning his back to her. She guessed he was explaining who she was because she could see the other man's eyes look towards her from time to time over his friend's shoulder.

She didn't mind their lack of overt friendliness, having long ago grown accustomed to country people's reserve, although she missed the old, easy companions in London who had dropped in at the studio at any time and had stayed talking half the night. Apart from Lionel, she knew no one in the village really well, and now even he had withdrawn his friendship.

The landlord remembered her, though, and asked after Max. Before Max had become crippled, they had frequently spent the evening at the Feathers, where Max had built up a small circle of drinking companions, although even with them she had never felt totally at ease and none of them had bothered to call at the house since Max's illness. She realised there were too many differences dividing them: their own London background, Max's profession of artist, the isolation of the house from the main village, her own disinclination to join in village activities such as the Women's Institute or the Church Fellowship. It was largely their own fault that they had remained cut off from the local people.

'Max?' she replied. 'Oh, he's a bit better today.'

'Glad to hear it,' the landlord said. 'And what can I get you?'

'I'd like a bottle of red wine, please, if you've got one.'

It took time. The keys to the cellar had to be detached from their hook, the cellar unlocked and the bottle found. Carrying it back into the bar, the landlord noticed it was dusty and took it away again to wipe it.

Nina didn't mind. She was used to slow service in the village shop. While she waited, she studied the collection of beer mats pinned up on the wall behind the counter and patted the head of the landlord's labrador which came from behind the bar to examine her, turning its ears inside out to expose the pinkish inner skin and the delicate whorls of the openings, fringed with fine, pale hairs. She thought of Danny, too, who must have become accustomed to the place during the few days he had stayed in the village, and she wondered what he was doing at that moment. Probably, like her, he was standing at the bar of some pub, only in London, perhaps the one in which she had treated herself to a lunchtime sandwich and a drink on her way to Zoe's that Tuesday. It seemed a lifetime away.

The sun had sunk by the time she had paid for the bottle and could leave. Propping it up carefully in the basket, she looked up at the sky. Strictly speaking, it was after lighting-up time, but she didn't want to walk home. It would take nearly a quarter of an hour.

In the end, she compromised by scooting the bike along the edge of the road, keeping one foot on the grass verge, so that if the local bobby happened to pass she could argue with some justification that she hadn't actually been riding. The bottle wobbled about in the basket, its head nodding this way and that. It had come up ice-cold from the cellar, too chilled to drink straight away, but if she drew the cork and stood it on top of the boiler, it ought to be warmed through by the time they were ready to eat. The price had been exorbitant, too, far more than an ordinary off-licence would charge, and she decided that if Max asked for the change she'd tell him she'd treated herself to a gin and tonic. That way, she'd avoid any fuss.

'Max!' she called out when, having put her bike away, she entered the kitchen. 'Max, I've got a bottle, but it's . . .'

She stopped in the doorway. The kitchen was empty. The basket chair still stood where she had last seen it, facing the door, but Max wasn't seated in it. There was only his cushion lying on the seat.

Her first reaction was exasperation. The old fool! He must have been taken short and tried to go to the lavatory on his own. Dumping down the bottle on the table, she started towards the door that led into the hall, but halted before she had taken more than a pace. There were unfamiliar objects on the table which had not been there when she had left for the Feathers. In the space where she had left the chopping board, pushed aside to make room for it, was Max's big, japanned box of paints, which she had last seen in the sideboard cupboard in the dining-room, its top tray full of squeezed-out tubes of paint lifted out and lying separately to expose the bottom section in which was a muddle of brushes, broken sticks of charcoal and paint-smeared rags. Beside it was a heap of washing, including the sheets from the caravan which she had intended ironing but hadn't yet got round to doing and which had been bundled away on Max's wheel-chair. The chair itself had gone from its accustomed corner.

But neither the presence of the box nor the absence of the chair alarmed her as much as the sight of the envelope, addressed to her, which was propped up against the box. It had been folded in half and was badly creased, as if it had been kept in Max's trouser pocket.

Even before she tore it open and read it, she knew where she would find him and, throwing aside the two sheets of paper, she set off at a stumbling run across the lawn where the cedar tree stood muttering to itself just as Max had described it, its layered branches keeping up a harsh, whispered conversation.

He was sitting in the wheel-chair in the summer-house,

facing out towards the darkening lawn where Lilith had last appeared to him, the gun lying on the wooden boards below his right hand, which hung down over the arm of the chair, his index finger extended as if pointing it out to her.

Thank God, she thought absurdly, his head's undamaged.

It was tipped back as if in slumber, the thick, white hair a little rumpled, the formidable nose jutting upwards but the expression on the face serene. He might have fallen asleep in the middle of some pleasant reverie.

She did not touch him, apart from pulling up the rug to cover the wound in his chest, and when she had completed that ministration she took his hand and laid it against her lips.

It was the kind of farewell Max would have preferred, without any fuss or histrionics; just a simple parting with the briefest physical contact between them and no words spoken, as, in the same manner the day before, he had taken her hand and laid it against his heart; his own gesture of farewell, as she now realised.

Finch found her sitting in the kitchen when, having knocked and received no answer, he let himself in, Boyce at his heels.

One look at her face was enough to tell him what had happened.

'Where is he?' he asked.

She gestured towards the garden.

'In the summer-house.'

Boyce nodded in answer to Finch's unspoken instruction and left the room, while the Chief Inspector drew up a chair beside her.

'He left a letter explaining everything,' Nina said and passed a sheet of paper to him.

'You had no idea?' Finch asked gently, taking it from her but making no attempt to read it.

She shook her head.

'None. I was afraid it was Danny. When did you realise the truth?'

'Only a short while ago.' He got up from the table and began preparing tea, putting the kettle on to boil and finding cups and saucers, so that their conversation assumed an almost laconic quality, he pottering about with the slightly disengaged air of a man occupied with a simple, domestic task, Nina listening and following his movements with her eyes, occasionally indicating where he could find the things he needed. 'I went to see your father and aunt this afternoon.'

'How were they?' she asked with an automatic response.

'Quite well. Your father's getting old, of course. It was your aunt who told me about your mother running away from home soon after she was married. It was then I made the connection.'

He did not want to admit that it had been one of Max's drawings of Lilith, tucked away among the other papers in the deed-box, which had first given him the clue to the relationship between Max and Nina's mother. Nina had quite clearly never seen it, and he felt it was one of those family secrets which he had no right to betray.

'With Lilith?' Nina was asking, and he was taken aback by the directness with which she met his eyes.

'Yes.'

'I had no idea myself until I read Max's letter. It seems unbelievable and yet, I suppose, once you realise they'd met, the rest had to follow. Like Max's exhibition.'

She was speaking in the kind of conversational shorthand which only people who have known each other for years normally use, in which superfluous explanation is omitted, but Finch could follow exactly what she meant. Once you accepted the basic premise of Max's affair with Nina's mother, her own meeting with Max and their subsequent relationship became inevitable, because he had sought her out in the same way as Eustace Quinn, having acquired some of Max Gifford's sketches, came looking for him.

'Where did they meet?' he asked. 'London?'

He had been forced to make that assumption, as Danny had been uncertain where his mother had gone during that brief separation, although he had been able to supply the date, September 1936.

'Yes. Max explains in his letter. She went to a hotel in Gower

Place, quite close to the art school where Max was teaching at the time. They met in the street one afternoon. Max stopped her and asked if she'd act as his model. It was the sort of thing he often did. They fell in love with each other almost at once. Max had a friend who rented a studio in Bloomsbury and they used to go there. She was afraid, if Max ever exhibited the portraits, that someone might recognise her, which was why he always painted her with her face hidden although, knowing him, I don't think that was the only reason. She was Lilith, his secret love, and he didn't want to share her with anyone. And then, she left him to go back to my father. Max didn't say why.'

'Her own mother was dying,' Finch explained.

'Who told you that?'

'Your aunt.'

'How strange! She never spoke to me about my mother except to make little hurtful remarks about her. I wonder why she told you.'

Finch carried the teapot over to the table, using this as an excuse not to reply. He did not want to have to explain that it had slipped out during an outburst directed against Nina herself, the outpourings of a lonely, embittered woman who could no longer hold back the dislike she had nurtured for so long against her niece.

'There's something else I don't understand,' Nina continued. 'How did Max find out our address? My parents had moved parishes, you see, shortly before I was born, and Max can't have had any idea where we were living. He says in his letter that she went away and he didn't know where she had gone.'

'The church was vandalised. Do you remember? There were reports in some of the London papers. I assume Max read one of them and recognised the surname. He must have known enough of Lilith's background to realise she was the wife of a country vicar, so he made the connection. The newspaper reports came out in June and shortly afterwards he arrived in the next village.'

'And he came looking for her?'

'Yes. So when you met it wasn't entirely coincidental. He found out that Lilith had died several years before, which must have shocked him. But what he really hadn't bargained for was the fact that he would fall in love with her daughter.'

It was Nina, thank God, who put into words the next part of the story.

'It wasn't true he was my father. That part of the letter is crazy!'

'But that's what he thought,' Finch said quietly. 'He worked out the dates, and it must have seemed possible that Lilith was carrying his child when she left him.'

'The silly old fool!' Nina's voice was full of exasperated tenderness. 'Even though neither Zoe nor I had children, it never seemed to occur to him that he was sterile. I suppose it would have hurt his pride to admit it. He was Max, the great lover, the great painter. He had to be able to create life as well as pictures. I could have told him the truth if he'd asked, but we never spoke about it. There was a lot of things we never discussed; it's too late now.'

'Didn't it occur to you to ask why he would never agree to marry you, which, of course, given the relationship he thought there was between you, he couldn't do?'

She looked at him with the same baffled exasperation, surprised at his obtuseness.

'No. Max said he didn't want to, and that was that. I just accepted it. Anyway, it didn't seem important. We were as good as legally married and I knew he'd never leave me.'

She smiled with secret satisfaction, remembering the day when Max had placed the crown of flowers on her head, a ceremony performed in front of witnesses which had been infinitely more hallowed and binding than any words mumbled over them in some London Registry Office. Not understanding the reason, Finch wondered at the strength of her conviction.

'And that's why Quinn had to die,' he continued in the same conversational voice. 'He was asking too many questions, and Max was afraid he'd find out the truth. Did he explain that part to you?'

'Yes. Evidently Eustace Quinn spoke to Max about it on Thursday evening. They were talking alone in the sitting-room. He told Max that he'd found out a bit about his life and it was his relationship with me that had first given him the idea. He told Max it was a good story and he knew a television producer who was interested in making a play out of it. It was to be broadcast at the same time as the exhibition was put on. That way, they'd get maximum publicity and Max's work would fetch top prices. Eustace Quinn even talked about going down to Heversham and interviewing Dad and Aunt Connie to get what he called "local colour". I think Max was afraid he'd find out the truth if he started asking questions.'

As he might very well have done, Finch thought, if, like him, he'd come across the Lilith sketch in Miss Webb's possession; which, no doubt, she'd found among her sister-in-law's private papers after her death and added to her own collection of documents proving betrayal. It had shown Lilith, dressed only in a petticoat, with her arms uplifted as she coiled that magnificent dark hair into a coronet on top of her head. As in the other drawings, her face had been hidden, but Miss Webb could have had no difficulty in recognising who had posed for it. Max must have known, or at least suspected, that Lilith owned the drawing; he might even have given it to her as a keepsake before they parted. And, with Eustace Quinn planning on making his own inquiries at Heversham, it gave Max a powerful enough motive for murder.

Nina was making a little grimace of disgust.

'He told Max he'd wake up and find he was famous overnight. "Instant success" was the way he put it. God! It makes me angry enough to want to kill him myself when I think of the years Max struggled to make a name for himself, and yet only a handful of people have ever heard of him.'

'Did you know Quinn had already bought up quite a few of Max's paintings on the quiet?'

'No, but it doesn't surprise me,' she replied, her voice hard. 'I warned him that Eustace Quinn would drive a hard bargain. It was part of the deal, of course. No television play, no exhibition.

Max had to choose. He decided instead to kill him on Thursday evening. He was afraid if I found out the truth about Lilith, I'd leave him. But even if I'd known, it wouldn't have made any difference. Max should have realised that.'

'So you don't think that was the real motive?' Finch asked, surprised at the implication.

'It was a large part of it. Max was growing old, you see, and was losing his self-confidence. Perhaps I was to blame for that. I let him see that there were days when I was tired of looking after him. But, for God's sake, he should have known me better than to believe I would ever leave him.'

Her anger flashed up briefly, directed partly at Max but mostly against herself. But she did not add, as she might have done, that Max's motive for murdering Quinn must have stemmed also from his own deeply felt bitterness and resentment that, after a lifetime of devotion to his art, he would be recognised, not so much as a painter, but as a character from a television play designed to fictionalise his love affair with a schoolgirl. In its way, it was as crude as Boyce's attitude to the artist's life-style.

Finch had finished his own tea. Nina's was only half drunk and the rest was going cold. He refilled their cups before asking the next question in a voice that was almost casual.

'How did he do it, Nina?'

Neither of them found his use of her Christian name in any way unusual. Seated with her at the table, he had again assumed the role of family friend, only this time there was nothing unnatural about it and she accepted it as real.

'He shot himself.'

'Do you know where he got the gun from?'

'It belonged to Zoe. God knows how she got hold of it, but before she met Max she used to have a lot of lovers; perhaps one of them gave it to her. All I know is she threatened Max with it once years ago and he took it off her. He must have kept it hidden in here.' She indicated the lower section of the paint-box with its jumble of rags and brushes. 'I don't know why he hung onto it, but Max was always secretive about some things.

Perhaps he liked it because it was a symbol of male power. He sometimes said a paintbrush was feminine. It was the equivalent of a woman's embroidery needle.'

A gun was also a phallic symbol, Finch thought, although he said nothing, merely nodding encouragingly to her to continue.

'He must have fetched the box when I was at the Feathers buying a bottle of wine. It was Max's idea I should go. I can see now that he had it all planned out. It was the first day he felt strong enough to get up, you see, after . . .'

For a moment her voice faltered, and she didn't finish the sentence. Finch completed the phrase 'after murder' silently to himself as Nina added, 'He must have got himself into the wheel-chair and pushed himself into the dining-room. God knows when he wrote the letter. This morning, perhaps, or last night. It would have taken him ages, because he can hardly hold a pen. He insisted on getting himself dressed, so it must have been then when he put it in his pocket. I didn't see him do it. I'm still not sure how he managed to get to the summer-house across the grass.'

Finch had his own theory about this, which he had no intention of explaining to her. Instead, he finished his tea and got to his feet.

'I'm going to have a word with my sergeant. I shan't be long. Among other things, I want to arrange to have your brother brought over here.'

Her face immediately became full of eagerness as well as anxiety.

'Danny! You've found him in London? Oh, God, is he all right?'

'Yes, perfectly. We brought him back to headquarters for questioning, but I'll make sure that he's released and I'll order a car to drive him straight here.'

He left it at that. Danny himself could explain exactly what had happened.

'I'll have to get a bed and a meal ready for him!' she cried.

As he left, she was already on her feet, clearing the table of their used cups.

Outside, Finch stood in the yard and, taking Max Gifford's letter from his pocket, he tipped it towards the light which fell through the curtained kitchen window. It was a single sheet of paper, carrying that day's date but no other superscription, an omission which made him suspect that there had been another letter addressed to Nina that she had not shown him. If he asked, she would no doubt deny its existence. Besides, what was the point? What he had in his hands was sufficient.

It read, in an awkward, painful handwriting as if Max Gifford had found difficulty in holding the pen:

'I killed Eustace Quinn because I was afraid he was going to find out the truth about Nina's mother. I called her Lilith but her real name was Margaret Webb. I met her in London in 1936 when she had run away from her husband. We became lovers, but after a few weeks she left me to return home, I didn't know where.

'In 1953, I discovered her address and went to find her, only to learn she had died about eight years before. While in the village, I met her daughter who, I had reason to believe, was also my child, a secret I have told no one.

'Eustace Quinn wanted to make the story of my relationship with Nina into a television play which would be broadcast at the same time as the exhibition. He made it clear that one would depend on the other and that I would have to sign a contract permitting the facts to be used as a basis for the plot.

'He told me this on Thursday evening when we were alone together and I decided then that I would have to kill him. He came the following morning after I had arranged for Nina to be out of the house. I was genuinely in pain, but I also knew that there were only a few tablets left. At my request, Quinn helped me downstairs to the kitchen where I struck him with the flat-iron which was used to prop open the door. I then lifted his body into the wheel-chair and moved it to the wash-house before returning to bed.

'I have decided to kill myself rather than face old age in prison. It is the cleanest way out. Nina knows nothing either of

Quinn's murder or of my intention to commit suicide. She is entirely innocent of both.'

It was signed M.G. in the same manner in which he had initialled the sketches of Lilith, the tail of the letter G curling back to encompass the M.

Having read it, Finch replaced it in his pocket. He was more than ever convinced that Max had written another letter, intended only for Nina, for she had referred to details of Max's relationship with Lilith which were not included in this account.

This one, his official statement, was short and factual, unemotional in its stark language, which did not attempt to excuse or even to explain more than the barest outline of what had happened. What agony Gifford had experienced in deciding on that double killing, Finch could only guess. But the memory of his face with its expression of utter exhaustion returned to the Chief Inspector's mind. Max Gifford had looked into the abyss of a personal hell and had been unable to contemplate its horrors any longer. At least, as he himself had stated, the alternative had the merit of a clean quietus which he had been able to control and in which some degree of self-respect had been possible.

Finch would not have wished it otherwise, a sentiment which he did not express to Boyce, whom he found pacing up and down the sunken lawn which faced the summer-house.

'I thought you were never coming,' he said, as he clambered up the bank to meet the Chief Inspector.

'You've had a look at him?' Finch asked, ignoring the complaint.

'Yes. He's been dead about an hour, I'd say. Shot through the heart, so he didn't stand any chance of surviving it. He'd undone his shirt to get to the right place, I assume.'

'Don't forget he was an artist. He'd know quite a lot about human anatomy,' Finch pointed out. 'Got a torch?'

'I fetched it from the car. Do you want to have a look at him?'

The beam caught the seated figure in its spotlight and illuminated also a restricted circle of rough planks, some still retaining the bark, of which the summer-house was made.

'Someone must have pulled the rug up over the wound,' Boyce added. 'I had to fold it back.'

Nina, Finch guessed. The rug was now lying across the lap, exposing the broad chest with the wound, dark with blood, on the left-hand side, like a mouth set agape.

Moving the torch downwards, Finch shone it onto the gun which was lying on the boards.

'A 1910 Mauser automatic; 635 millimetre; takes a rimless ammunition,' Boyce said with the quick but deliberately off-hand knowledge of the expert. He fancied himself as something of a specialist in guns, those macho symbols of the phallus, the strong, thrusting extension of the body that ejaculated death. 'Probably brought back by someone who'd served in the First World War as booty captured off a prisoner. It's a German officer's side-arm. But how the hell did he get himself here?'

It was the same question that Nina had asked, and this time Finch offered an explanation.

'Nina helped him downstairs as he couldn't make it alone. She had no idea, of course, what was in his mind. After he'd sent her out on the pretext of buying a bottle of wine, he must have got himself into the wheel-chair, which he could have managed on his own. Nina Gifford told me at the start of the investigation that he could walk a few steps by himself if he'd got something to hold on to. Besides, it's incredible what physical strength even a cripple can produce if he has to. My guess is that he propelled himself as far as the edge of the lawn and then pushed the chair from there, using it as a support. He couldn't have got it across the rough grass in any other way. And don't forget, he'd already done much the same with Quinn's body.'

Earlier that evening, Finch had already gone over that part of the theory with Boyce, how Quinn, having arrived at Althorpe House, had gone upstairs to find Max, as arranged, and had helped him down to the kitchen where Max had killed him. At the time, he had not known what weapon had been used, but Max Gifford's letter had now made that clear. The flat-iron was not only to hand but was also the right shape with its blunted edge. And it was heavy enough to crack anybody's spine.

What happened after that had been, in effect, a dummy run for his own subsequent suicide. The body had been lifted into the wheel-chair and Max Gifford, clinging to the wheel-chair's handle, had pushed it across the yard to the outhouse, not daring to leave the body in the kitchen, as suspicion would almost certainly have been directed immediately towards him, for he could not have failed to be aware of a murder taking place inside the house. As Finch had pointed out to Boyce, the fact that the murderer had obliterated the marks on the wash-house floor should have put him on to Max Gifford much earlier. It wasn't footprints that he had been so anxious to get rid of but the tell-tale double line of grooves where the wheels of the chair had run across the dust.

How the hell he had got himself upstairs again, Finch could only guess. It must have taken a superhuman effort to drag himself from one tread to the next. It was no wonder that it had been three days before he had recovered from the exhaustion and that when Finch had interviewed him he had appeared an old, sick man. Finch was, however, in no doubt that Max Gifford had planned the murder as carefully as his own suicide. On both occasions, he had made sure that Nina was out of the house, sent away on some pretext: on the first, to fetch medicine from the doctor's, on the second, to buy a bottle of wine. The only mistake he had made was to mention to Nina that Quinn had spoken of a partner, which, in turn, she had passed on to the Chief Inspector, thereby leading him to investigate Quinn's contacts and finally to establish his connection with Lawford. Quinn's own inquiries into Nina Gifford's past, through Danny and Blanche, had already made Finch suspect that Quinn's curiosity extended beyond normal business practice, although he had assumed at first that it was only Nina in whom Quinn had been interested. Once the link between Nina, Lilith and Max had been made, Lawford's role could be deduced, although if Max Gifford had remained silent about Quinn's partner, Finch would have remained totally in the dark.

Had it been a genuine mistake, or had Gifford deliberately let fall that one small, significant piece of information in an attempt, perhaps, to hint at the truth or even to give Finch a sporting chance of discovering it? It was a question that could never now be answered, though he preferred to think that the latter alternative was the correct one.

Out loud, he said, 'Well, there's nothing more we can do here, Tom. Get on the car radio and call up McCullum and Pardoe. We'll need an ambulance, too, and a couple of DCs to give a hand generally. Kyle and Marsh will do.' Suddenly he changed his mind. 'No, make that Kyle and Cunningham. It's about time that young recruit had a taste of violent death. And while you're at it, arrange for a car to bring Danny Webb over here. We've got no reason to hold him any longer, and Nina Gifford's going to need someone to be with her.'

'Will do,' Boyce replied. 'Where'll you be? Here?'

'No. I don't think Max Gifford will be needing my company. I'll be at the house with her.'

She had been crying, he realised, when he re-entered the kitchen. Her face was swollen and blotched, the face of a woman who has recently wept, and her movements were heavy and languid. But pride prevented her from breaking down again in front of him; or perhaps she had no more tears to shed.

'I'll stay with you until Danny arrives,' he offered. 'That is, if you'd like me to.'

'Please. Will it take long?'

He knew she did not mean just Danny's arrival, but also that of the police, who were to take Max's body away.

'About an hour,' he told her. 'Possibly less. Is there anything I can do in the meantime?'

She answered so quickly that he guessed she had thought it out already.

'Yes, there is. Could you help me take down the picture over Max's bed? It's too heavy for me to manage on my own.'

'Of course.'

He followed her upstairs, wondering what she planned to do with it, but when he had manhandled it down from the wall, all she said was, 'Turn it round, please, so I can't see it.'

He propped it up under the window so that the canvas back was showing, permitting himself only the briefest of glances at it as he did so. Not that he could see much at such close quarters. The portrait was reduced to a mere chiaroscuro of swirls and daubs of colour, pink, red, black, flesh-tinted, the pigment standing out proud in places above the flat surface like a contour map of the body, following the landscape of the flesh.

After he had moved it into position, he drew the curtains across the window. That way, she would not see his men about their task when they arrived.

'What will you do now?' he asked her later when they had returned to the kitchen. They were drinking tea again; she had made it herself this time, with an abstracted air, as if only half her mind was on the task.

'I don't really know. I haven't really thought about it, except I shan't stay here. I couldn't bear it. I suppose I shall sell the place and move back to London, although I can't imagine it will fetch much.'

'Oh, I don't know,' Finch put in. 'The land alone must be worth quite a bit.'

'But the house needs a lot spending on it.'

'Could be,' he agreed vaguely.

She made no further comment, although Finch could have added the ending to that particular story. She would buy, or possibly lease, a flat in London and Danny would move in with her. It had, he thought wryly, the inevitability of a fairy-story. 'And they lived happily ever after.'

God help her!

Danny arrived before the ambulance. Finch heard the car draw up in the yard and guessed, by the impatient slamming of its door, who it was who had come.

Getting up, he crossed the kitchen. Nina had guessed, too. She had risen to her feet in order to be ready to greet him, her arms already lifted in a gesture of welcome, her face trans-figured, and as he passed Danny on the doorstep he heard her cry out loud,

'Danny! Oh, thank God you're here!'

Supervising the photographing and the removal of Max Gifford's body kept his mind busy, and it was only when he returned to the yard, following the men who were carrying the stretcher to the waiting ambulance, that he allowed himself to think of her again.

Pausing in the yard, he glanced across at the lighted kitchen window, its curtains drawn against the outside world, and thought there would be no more home-comings for Max Gifford. Nor, come to that, for himself.

A selection of bestsellers from SPHERE

FICTION

FULL CIRCLE	Danielle Steel	£2.25 ☐
SUMMER SONG	Pamela Oldfield	£2.25 ☐
THE AMTRAK WARS VOLUME 2:		
FIRST FAMILY	Patrick Tilley	£2.25 ☐
DELCORSO'S GALLERY	Philip Caputo	£2.25 ☐
THE BRITISH CROSS	Bill Granger	£1.95 ☐

FILM & TV TIE-INS

THE RIVER	Steven Bauer	£1.95 ☐
INDIANA JONES AND THE LOST		
TREASURE OF SHEBA	Rose Estes	£1.25 ☐
THE WHALE TALE	John Stevenson	95p ☐
BEST FRIENDS	Jocelyn Stevenson	£1.50 ☐

NON-FICTION

EDWINA	Richard Hough	£2.95 ☐
KITTY CAMPION'S HANDBOOK OF		
HERBAL HEALTH	Kitty Campion	£2.95 ☐
TALKING TO MYSELF	Anna Raeburn	£1.95 ☐
A JOBBING ACTOR	John Le Mesurier	£1.95 ☐
AROUND THE WORLD IN 78 DAYS		
	Nicholas Coleridge	£1.95 ☐

All Sphere books are available at your local bookshop or newsagent, or can be ordered direct from the publisher. Just tick the titles you want and fill in the form below.

Name _____

Address _____

_____

Write to Sphere Books, Cash Sales Department, P.O. Box 11, Falmouth, Cornwall TR10 9EN

Please enclose cheque or postal order to the value of the cover price plus:

UK: 55p for the first book, 22p for the second book and 14p for each additional book ordered to a maximum charge of £1.75.

OVERSEAS: £1.00 for the first book plus 25p per copy for each additional book.

BFPO & EIRE: 55p for the first book, 22p for the second book plus 14p per copy for the next 7 books, thereafter 8p per book.

Sphere Books reserve the right to show new retail prices on covers which may differ from those previously advertised in the text or elsewhere, and to increase postal rates in accordance with the PO.